THE
BURNING
MAGUS

DON ALLMON

RIPTIDE
PUBLISHING

Riptide Publishing
PO Box 1537
Burnsville, NC 28714
www.riptidepublishing.com

The Burning Magus

Cover art: Simoné, dreamarian.com
Editor: Sarah Lyons
Layout: L.C. Chase, lcchase.com/design.htm

ISBN: 978-1-62649-756-6

First edition
November, 2018

Also available in ebook:
ISBN: 978-1-62649-755-9

THE
BURNING
MAGUS

DON ALLMON

TABLE OF
CONTENTS

CHAPTER ONE

The confessional smelled of fresh-cut cedar, the church was that new. The window separating Austin Shea from the priest slid open, *snap*. A golden cloth screen kept the priest obscured: nothing but the vaguest hint of a silhouette through the tiny gaps in the threads, even to Austin's elven eyes.

"Bless me, for I have sinned. It has been six years, four months, and four days since my last confession."

6-4-4 was the code. There was no response for long seconds. The wrong priest might have taken his strangely precise dating as disrespecting the sacrament, and a scolding was coming. The right priest, on the other hand . . .

"You should not be here." Mother Minerva's voice was the liquid purr of a chocolate cat. And now that he knew it was her, he thought he could feel the calming warm brandy of her glamour. It was a good glamour for an elven priest to have.

"I got a job, a big one. The kind that makes a reputation. I need some help."

"I should say so. But not from me."

"It's a hit on a wizard's castle. Rescue operation. Stealthy, smart. Sneak in. Sneak out. All tracks covered." He downplayed the job as if it were any old castle they were raiding and not Alcatraz Island; as if it were any wizard they were hitting and not Firelight, whose patron was a dragon; and as if it were any prisoner they were freeing and not an AI with a scientifically impossible elfish glamour, made doubly priceless because that AI had been made from the memories of Austin's murdered sister. "I need a geek, a ninja, and a wizard. A metamorphic or a water wiz would be good. Is Ortez available?"

"No one is available."

"Jenny Hatchett or Penthesilea Logan?"

"No one."

"Are they fighting again?" Jenny and Penth were always fighting. "How about—"

"No one will work with you, Austin."

"Is this about money? The job pays. It pays real good." Which was a lie. He had nothing to pay anyone. He'd cross that bridge later.

"It's not about money."

"Everything's about money."

"All right, yes. It is about money. The answer's still no."

"Did you not hear the part where I said 'the kind of job that makes a reputation'? We're talking job of a lifetime here. You heard I got JT with me, right? We're together again."

Together again. Well, they were speaking and fucking and working with each other, so that counted as "together," didn't it? Just like old times.

"We're together again," he repeated, as if repeating it made it more true. He could repeat it as many times as he had breath; it still wouldn't make them together the way he wanted them to be. "People should be lining up to work with us."

"You have a bounty on you. You're *persona non grata.*"

"I've had a goddamn bounty on my head for years and—" His volume had gone up along with his frustration. She shushed him. "—and it hasn't been a problem yet."

"The bounties before have been token complaints. Feathers in your cap, quite honestly. Bragging rights. They've never been serious. These are serious."

"Who placed the bounty?"

"Who *didn't* place one? Lisa Kuang-Li, Mountain Head of the Electric Dragon Triad, has put up two hundred million for software theft, property damage, and the murder of two dozen of her people."

"They shot first. That's not murder, that's self-defense."

"Reportedly, you stole from them first."

"Technically that was Buzz, not me. How come he doesn't have a bounty?"

"He does. His is two hundred fifty million."

"Buzz's bounty is more than mine?" That hardly seemed fair.

"The druids of Boise have offered fifty million for the return of an artifact you stole from them."

And that pissed him off even more. "Those fuckers. I didn't steal nothing. It was *mine*!" The unicorn horn had technically belonged to his grandfather, but his grandfather had gone and left it sitting right there on the mantel, so that hardly counted as theft.

He'd gotten loud again, and she shushed him again. "And there are others. You've been very busy over the last few weeks. If you worked half as hard making friends as you do making enemies . . ."

"Blah blah blah." He waved his hands dismissively though she couldn't see them. "You sound just like Buzz. And JT. And everyone else. There's gotta be people who'll work with us."

"Oh, there are. Desperate and stupid people. I don't represent desperate and stupid people. I represent professionals."

"You've fixed me up for years."

"The only one I can fix you up with now is God. Would you like to confess your sins? The way your life is about to go, Austin Shea, I strongly advise it."

The stained glass windows of Our Lady of Avalon portrayed the Knights of the Round Table. The dust mote–scattered rainbow light made the place a fairyland, which wasn't far from the truth. The Church (capital C) wasn't comfortable with elves and orcs—too much bad history (never mind it was all fiction). Our Lady of Avalon was New Catholic. Their Pope was French and they traced their made-up lineage back to the Avignon Papacy. History was everyone's plaything these days.

Old elves and orcs—zero-generation Catholics no longer welcome in other churches—knelt scattered in pews. They prayed and lit candles in alcoves before unusual saints. At least everyone here knew the proper pronunciation of *Gawain*.

Would Mother Minerva sell him out? Was she online right now telling one old enemy or another, *He's here; come and get him. Remember my price*? She wouldn't really do that, would she?

Had Austin gone so far off the rails that Minerva would risk her reputation like that?

Maybe he had.

Two weeks ago Austin, JT, and Buzz had stolen a "ghost"—an AI fragment—from the Electric Dragon Triad and had shot up a block of Telegraph Hill and destroyed a druid's lodge in the process. And not two days later (though it wasn't their fault), a wizard had burned down a forest near Boise. So Austin had to admit they'd racked up a lot of ill will and bad karma in a very short time.

So maybe Minerva would risk her reputation. Hear his confession? Fuck that. Most likely Minerva had wanted to delay him a few minutes (hell, a few hours) so she could make her calls.

He should have run from there. He imagined Triad foot soldiers, 49ers, positioning themselves outside; cybernetic assassins in sniper nests; or druid-awakened rose bushes waiting to strangle him.

He didn't run. He would never run. He stopped at a shrine. He lit a candle for his sister, Roan. He knelt and prayed to Mary-called-Magdalene. It was a formless kind of prayer. He made no promises, no requests but hope, though hope for what, he was too superstitious to think.

What kind of faith was it when you were so assured of your own damnation you couldn't properly pray?

Outside, he wasn't mobbed by 49ers or shot by snipers. There were no bloodthirsty roses. He made it to the parking garage just fine. It would have been disappointingly dull if not for Diego.

The Corvette was parked just where Austin had left it: level three, hind-end first like an asshole parks, between an Audi and a BMW.

Diego Silva lounged against the front fender, both hands shoved deep in the pockets of his cream-colored mulberry silk trousers. His hair was as long and curled as a Bach cantata. It was tucked behind his elven ears. His eyes were dark and gently upturned like some elves' eyes did. He cocked his head one way and his shoulders the other, contrapposto, and pouted full glossy lips. He shrugged as if embarrassed to be found there. "You stole my car."

"I borrowed it. You gave me the key."

"'Borrow' is a few hours. It's been two weeks. I knew you wouldn't bring it back. I told myself, 'If you love someone, set them free.' That's what I told myself."

Diego spoke the same way he fucked: in a slow, accented drawl, like he'd learned both English and fucking in South Carolina. His glamour was exquisitely bitter, dizzying in small bites and trace quantities, sickening in anything more. Like radiation.

He slid a hand over the Corvette's curved fender. That touch would have made JT close his eyes, would have sent an electric spark through him that lit him up like a downtown Christmas. Austin ground his teeth. Touching the Corvette like that wasn't for Diego to do. It was for Austin to do.

"Well, since I'm set free . . ." He pulled out the fob and unlocked the car.

Diego wasn't a wizard. He had the same kind of built-in tech most people had. He locked it again with his mind. Austin should have known he could do that. The alarm and plasma field were off after all. Diego could have taken his car back anytime he'd wanted, but he'd waited here for Austin. That meant Diego didn't just want his car back; he wanted something else too.

Austin focused his attention on the garage. The lighting was poor. The ceiling was low. It was packed with cars jammed between concrete support columns. The floor sloped gently. That shadow there, that boot scuff there, that click of plastic against plastic from somewhere over there: telltale signs Diego had brought friends, the lurking-in-shadows kind of friends.

So it was vengeance he wanted.

Diego said, "A cynical man would think those weeks we spent together meant nothing to you. All you wanted was my money, my booze, my dick, my car, not in that order. All my friends told me so. I didn't believe them. I still don't. They're wrong about you. It's not like it looks. There was a good reason you took my car and didn't come back. Just tell me why, Austin, and I'll give you a second chance."

Okay, not vengeance. It was Austin himself Diego wanted.

Sometimes Austin was just a touch more amazing than he'd ever intended.

"I don't really need a second chance. Your friends were right."

"Prove it."

The car locks popped open as Austin pressed the key fob. "I'm trying to."

Pop. Diego locked it again. "Come here and kiss me. Kiss me and I'll know if you're lying or not."

He wanted to point out that Diego hadn't known the first five dozen times Austin had kissed him, so why was this time going to be any different?

For two weeks Austin had let Diego fuck him because Diego had a car that Austin needed, a car that would seduce an orc named JT. He supposed he could just do it again. Except it didn't seem as much fun this time around.

"Austin, I said kiss me."

Austin shuffled toward him, feigning shy apologetic reluctance.

Diego grabbed Austin by the hair, swung him around, and backed him into the Corvette, thighs against its arched fender. He kissed Austin bruisingly hard, all the bone and teeth behind soft flesh, tasting of the cigarettes Diego preferred, woody like an elf should taste, but burning.

Glamour, all eros and sensuality, Austin's tinged with a need to make it rough and Diego's bitter as a grudge, swept out from them in a wave. There were johns who paid good money to watch two elves fuck and feel the faerie wash of their sex-heightened glamour. Austin wondered how Diego's little gang of thugs hidden among the cars were handling it.

Diego crushed hard against him, pushing Austin's ass up on the fender and laying him down over the hood. Through thin trousers, Diego's long and slender cock ground against the inside of Austin's thigh. Inside Austin, it would shove up against his gut, deep as medieval impalement.

Diego fought with the zipper of his pants. "God, I love you. I've never met anyone like you."

Austin pawed back at him, sucked at his mouth, thinking the burning-cherry taste of Diego was a bit stale. "We should take this somewhere else," he said, wanting to delay.

"We're safe here." Diego smiled down at him. It should have been a perfectly beautiful smile. Tusks would have improved it.

But then Diego's smile faltered and dropped. He blinked. "What did you do to my car?"

Austin turned his head to follow Diego's gaze. The 'Vette was an odd shade of blacker-than-black meant to absorb radar. In the dim light of the garage, the edges and lines of the car were nearly invisible. Up close, Austin could see that the hood was dented and scarred like it had been through a hailstorm, scraped all to fuck.

Austin smiled, remembering how all that damage had gotten there.

"I . . ." The sound came out like a long croak as Austin scrambled for a lie that seemed believable. Aw, fuck all the lies. Lies were for people he cared about. "I fucked an orc on it."

"An orc?"

"Yeah, you know: Green? Muscles? Tusks? Big cock? Well, this one at least. Pathologically technologically inclined? Also this one; not a species thing."

"An orc?" Diego hissed in Austin's ear, still pressing him down. "You fucked one of those *things* on the hood of my car?"

And with that one word, Austin was going to end this here and now. Except he felt a small plastic circle press firm against his temple. Austin hadn't even noticed Diego's pistol, and it wasn't often Austin failed to notice something like that. Maybe he hadn't researched Diego Silva as thoroughly as he should have. It was possible Diego was more than an LA businessman.

"Let go of that knife, Austin."

Austin let go of the little knife he'd drawn. It clattered to the concrete floor. The sound rattled off the ceiling and pillars. He held his hands out, empty: no threat here.

Diego backed away, gun still on him. Six armed and armored people stepped out from behind cars and support pillars. They pointed assault rifles at Austin, fingers on triggers, which seemed an unnecessary escalation. They were a bit of a mess. Some had hard-ons. Austin could see them through their fatigues. The rest looked a little shaky. Shoulder patches said SecCorp, so these bodyguards were run-of-the-mill. They didn't even make Austin's blood pressure bump.

Austin sat upright and straightened his clothes. "His name is JT. He isn't a thing. And I gave him your car. It's not yours anymore. It's his." He pointed to the marks on the hood to prove his point.

Diego circled around him to the door of the 'Vette and sprang the lock. The door fanned up and out, and Diego slid into the seat where JT belonged. The door swept closed. The car came on. The window came down.

Diego said through it, "You know, I made a mistake. I forgot that when it comes to bad boys, you gotta tame 'em. Someday, Austin, you'll realize what you're missing. You'll come back to me, and I'll forgive you . . . if you beg long enough." He slipped on a pair of sunglasses, which was ridiculous because this was a parking garage in San Francisco. "You six. Tame him for me."

He smiled at Austin, bittersweet-sad, and said, "I'll see you around," because if nothing else, Diego wasn't an idiot, and he knew those mercs didn't stand a chance.

The car spun out of its spot, fishtailed a bit with an eye-watering smell of rubber on pavement, and then roared down the garage lane, ten times louder than it should be, squealing, echoing, squealing and squealing over slick concrete each turn to the exit.

The merc captain shouldered his gun, cracked his knuckles, and said, "You heard him, folks."

Austin sighed. If JT found out he killed six people and still lost the Corvette, well, he didn't even want to think of what the orc would do. This was gonna have to be bloodless. And right now bloodless was the last thing he wanted.

Austin sucked at a knuckle, skin broken, and watched the bus stops pass. He pulled the cord for the next one, not sure he knew what he was doing, but it was what everyone else had done. Austin could count the number of times he'd ridden on a city bus on one hand.

The bus stopped at the corner, sank, hissing, and Austin stepped onto the sidewalk hoping JT wasn't watching.

But he was. The orc was sitting at the table in the front window of Harvey's Bar & Grille. He was sitting frozen, pint of beer halfway to his lips, mouth all agape, tusks at funky angles, eyes on Austin. Those eyes tracked him past the window. None of the rest of him moved.

Christ.

Austin went in. Harvey's had seen better days. It did most of its business at three in the afternoon. There was a bit of a crowd, mostly humans, a few orcs, all of them down on their luck, the kind of crowd that didn't ask many questions and kept to themselves. There wasn't a single elf in the place other than him. He took a deep breath and told himself he was awesome, better than everyone, prepping himself for the inevitable glares.

He slid into the seat opposite JT. JT hadn't moved from his storefront pose: drink still tipped exactly so. "Did you just take the bus? Where's my car?"

"We got a problem."

"Yeah: Where's my car?"

"In the shop. Mother Minerva's blacklisted us."

"Blacklisted? What do you mean 'in the shop'?"

"Apparently we're on everyone's shit list. No one wants to be associated with us anymore."

JT set his glass down with a hard *clunk*. Beer sloshed over the rim, which meant he was annoyed. "*Us*, or *you*? *Shop*, Austin. Why is my car in the shop?"

It was best to stay calm and matter-of-fact. "The hood was all dented and scratched. It needed to be fixed."

"We can't do this job on our own. And you can't just take that car to a body shop." JT hissed extra quiet in case anyone was listening, "They record VINs. It'll flag the police. What are we gonna do?"

"It'll be fine."

"How do you know it'll be fine?"

"Because I know everything, all right?"

JT folded his arms, cocked his head, and rolled his eyes: triple-sarcasm. "'Everything' like where we're gonna get help without Minerva? Maybe I was gonna fix it."

"Well, now you don't need to. I know some wizards okay. Down-low wizards."

"'Down-low wizards'? Virgin fucking goddess! Maybe I wanted to fix it!"

"You're kind of loud." Austin signaled the bartender. She ignored him because he was an elf, so he sighed, and JT waved his hand in the air like ordering a beer was a spell. And goddamn it, she brought a beer over, but of course she didn't crack the cap for him, so Austin did it himself. He pulled JT's plate of un-eaten ketchup-drenched fries toward himself. Like all orcs, JT was a carnivore. He ate veggies when he had to. It was weird how many orcs thought French fries were meat. It was doubly-weird how JT thought they became more like meat by spraying them with ketchup. Austin supposed it was the red that did it.

"Look, I'm sorry about the car, okay? I should have asked you first before taking it to a shop. I didn't know it would bother you so much."

"Well, it bothers me. That's my car."

Sometimes Austin had a good idea, like stealing the Corvette to win JT over. But he was so used to his ideas being awful that when they weren't, it was fucking magic. And he knew he'd fucked up by losing that car. And he felt bad about lying, but somehow that made it all the more important for the lie to work. "If you want, we can dent it again when we get it back."

JT pulled his Massey Ferguson ball cap off. His hair was cut short, lightning bolts shaved into the temples, except for his bangs. His bangs stuck out all directions, adorable and disheveled, and he swept a hand through them and made them worse.

"So do we need to scrap the plan and start over? It's kind of late to start over. The summer solstice is less than a month away. Solstice is a shitty time to do it anyway: a fire festival. All Firelight's wizards are going to be there. Probably Firelight too. Let's push the job back."

JT was a planner. Austin wasn't. Austin was perfectly fine with whatever plan JT decided upon. Austin took a fry from the plate and drew a picture in the ketchup, using it as a brush. Austin wasn't much of an artist; repertoire, limited. He painted balls and a cock.

JT went on, "But if we keep with the plan, we'll know where they are, no surprises, right, and they're all going to be busy reworking their magic, all their wards and protections and stuff, so half of those wards won't be working, so yeah, you're right, I agree, we stick with June 20. Good."

Austin had realized a long time ago that there was some version of himself that lived in JT's head, and it was that version that JT talked to at times, not the real Austin.

Austin pushed more ketchup around, elaborating. He squiggled some veins on the side of the cock. He corrected mistakes. That vein there wasn't quite that squiggly in real life. He sucked all the ketchup off a fry leaving it soggy and flaccid. He let it hang from his mouth until JT noticed, then slurped it in.

JT pretended to ignore him. He tugged his cap down. He tapped his beer bottle against one tusk, *tonk tonk tonk*. "Maybe we can do it ourselves. We got you and me, Buzz and Comet—and I know you're not happy with Comet, but Comet knows his shit."

The funny thing was: JT's head-version of Austin was better at being Austin than Austin was himself. Head-version knew all of real-life Austin's arguments and was better at defending them than real-life Austin could ever hope to do. It was like JT practiced arguing with Austin and had perfected it to an art, and Austin didn't even have to be there.

He wasn't sure if he liked that. But at least it meant that JT thought about him when Austin wasn't around, and he *did* like that.

"And Dante can drive, and *I'm* not happy with that, but you're right and she ain't gonna just sit around, so she might as well drive. So we can do it ourselves."

Austin chewed the slurped-in fry and nudged ketchup with a new fry-brush. It was a passable half-retracted foreskin.

"No, you're right, we can't do it ourselves. We still need a way to get to the island—a water wizard is best. And a way to get off the island if everything goes south—someone who makes a good distraction."

Austin cocked his head, studied his drawing.

"Okay, you take care of it. You know people, right? No goddamn down-low wizards! I mean good people? Somebody's gotta still like you, right? Yeah, that'll work. Okay, we're set. Same plan as before."

Austin nodded, satisfied with the plan (which was the same plan as before). He slid out of the booth and drank his beer in a long series of gulps, thumped his chest, belched loudly, and set the empty bottle down. "I'm glad we sorted that out."

JT squinted at the ketchup-painted cock and balls.

Austin said, "That's you. That's yours. It looks just like that, life-like, down to that squiggle there. If this was performance art, I'd squirt the whole bottle on the window. Ketchup come."

"What did you do to your hand?" JT had finally noticed the cut on his knuckle.

"I punched someone really hard. I got some ideas for help: a wizard and a distraction."

"How about an idea of how we're going to get home without a car."

"This is San Francisco, everything is ten blocks away, fucking walk. Except . . ." Austin pulled a paper ticket from his pocket and laid it in front of JT. "Bus pass. See? I think of everything." And Austin patted him on the back and left him there in that hopeless bar and grill with a plateful of bus pass and ketchup cock.

THE JOB THAT WENT BAD
PART 1

For an operations center, the inside of the Novadri Sportif appeared no different than any other minivan. All JT's modifications were under the dash and hood.

JT was driver and lookout. He did the lookout part via a half dozen drones. He swiveled his seat left and right and checked the VI software he'd installed on the drones. He cycled through all the cameras he'd placed around the research lab over the past week: alleys, rooftops, and freight entrances. The place seemed abandoned. Their informants said it wasn't.

Sitting next to him, Roan picked at her lower lip with red nails, a habit that meant she was concentrating and deep in the net. JT glanced over her virtual shoulder and the network bloomed into life, geometric and Gibsonian. He saw the steady midnight trickle of traffic he expected: lab systems asking centralized network resources for patch updates, mail, messaging, and file transfers. Nothing out of the ordinary. The lab was asleep, data flow a soft snore.

In the back of the Sportif, Austin ran magic-loaded rocks along broadhead edges, transferring the power from stone to arrow and reducing each stone to a pile of dust in the process. The rocks Austin used were virgin, untouched by human hands (except his own, which were very definitely not virgin). How magic accumulated in them, JT didn't know. Austin said they were spirit poop. Who knew? It was a weird enough world.

Across from Austin, Grayson checked his link to his armor and ran through combat protocols. JT used to watch Mexican soap operas to practice his Spanish. There was one, *Hijas de perdición*, where a rakish stranger seduced each of a powerful family's daughters in turn before being caught in flagrante delicto by the family matriarch. Show finale, he was taken out back and pulled apart by horses. Gruesome. He came back in a follow-up show. Turned out he was a devil sent to make the family pay for their sins or something.

Grayson could have played that devil. He was darkly beautiful, moody in the best of times, angry all the rest. He was tolerable because he didn't talk much, kept to himself, and he was fantastic at his job, which was killing people. Roan said he was also a fantastic fuck, like a whole other person when you got him alone, still just as quiet but gentle as a lamb. JT could hardly imagine.

"What are you going to do with your share of the loot?" Austin asked, pre-job patter meant to take the edge off.

"Gonna buy a Corvette," JT said. He always said some car.

"A Corvette? That's a trash car." Austin always criticized his choice.

"Yeah, but not the one I want. Next year's Dawnstrike. Limited edition. Sexy as fuck. Six hundred on the magway. Full sensory integration on the exterior. You could fuck it in the tailpipe, and I'd feel it like it was mine."

"What's a tailpipe?"

JT sighed, unsure if Austin was teasing or really didn't know. "Old combustion engine tech. Never mind. It's just a figure of speech."

Roan, still half-submerged in data, said dreamily, "I'm getting a kitten."

"Oooh!" JT said. "One of the shrunk-down genetic lions? Those things are cool." Miniature lions were all the rage.

"No, just a normal kitten."

"What brand?" Austin said.

"It's *breed*, Austin, not *brand*. Any breed. A rescue kitten, whatever they got."

"Those cost about a dollar. What are you going to do with the rest of the money?"

"Buy her a diamond necklace."

Austin said, "I'm going to pay Riley Chan's to close to the public so it's just me and every piece of clothing Angeline Donadieu and Zoe Gianfonté have ever designed. I'm going to try on everything while a dozen naked sales clerks give me blowjobs and serve me champagne with diamonds in the glass."

"Diamonds are my thing," Roan said. Roan didn't own any diamonds that JT knew of. Her jewelry was plain and gold-plated.

"There's enough diamonds in the world; we can both do diamonds."

They all waited for Grayson to play along with the game, knowing he wouldn't (but that was part of the game too). The silence lingered, the clicking and snaps of Grayson tightening his armor grew more and more pointed. Finally—satisfyingly—he said, "You people waste oxygen. This ain't a fucking game. And there ain't no money."

They all went back to their preparations. Austin snuck up alongside JT and whispered (as if everyone wasn't right there), "Let's go. Five minutes."

"No," JT said. "He's right, this isn't a game." They were here to save a bunch of kids' lives. It wasn't the kind of thing they usually did. It wasn't the kind of thing they *ever* did. And it was making him edgy. It was one thing to joke around when it was just you and your friends in danger, but joking around when there were innocent lives on the line didn't feel right.

"C'mon. Five minutes. You'll feel better."

"I feel fine."

"No, you don't. You're edgy."

"I'm checking my drones."

"How many times have you run that check?"

"Five."

"Five means you're edgy. C'mon."

Austin popped the door and dropped to the street outside.

JT'd had four years to acclimate to Austin's and Roan's glamour, and he still couldn't tell when what he felt was him or them. An elf's glamour bloomed when they went into puberty. Evolutionists said it was a mating advantage. JT loathed evolutionists. Orcs and elves hadn't evolved, the zero-generation had just appeared overnight—part of the great magical Awakening—and genetic theories didn't matter for shit. An elf's glamour was always sensual if not sexual, each one flavored just a little bit differently. And for whatever reason, orcs felt glamours more sharply than humans or other elves.

Roan's glamour—each of her gestures, the smell of her, the sound of her voice—reminded JT of old near-miss boyfriends: the academic on the bus with his ancient pulp novels who JT crushed on but never spoke to; a fireman after a local fire struggling to repack his hose in a way that had made JT think dirty thoughts he'd never been brave enough to act on. Roan's glamour turned JT introspective and melancholy. No, not *turned*, because JT had always been thoughtful and prone to moods. A glamour took what was already there and magnified it. Roan's glamour encouraged him, told him it was okay to be what he was. He liked Roan's glamour.

—*Jesus, fucking go*, Roan sent. —*You two are pathetic. And he's driving me crazy.*

Austin's glamour made him horny and set him on edge. Around Austin, if he wasn't careful, if he didn't calm himself with deep breaths from time to time, he'd use more strength for everything than he needed: he'd hold coffee cups more tightly, turn bolts until threading stripped, bite when he fucked. And no, he couldn't blame all that on Austin no more than he could blame his moodiness on Roan. (Though he blamed Austin anyway because it was easy to blame Austin for everything.) But the truth was, Austin would have made JT horny even without the glamour. JT liked to bite when he fucked no matter who it was. The glamour made those urges nearly irresistible—just like they did now.

He followed Austin. Outside, cool fog enveloped them. They walked around to the sidewalk side, and with barely a glance to see if anyone was watching, Austin dropped to his knees.

JT unzipped and flopped himself free, dick and balls both. JT was horse-hung and bull-balled. He was touchy about it. Orcs were always judged by their bodies: Big and scary, and therefore dumb as fuck. Goddess, he hated that. His dick was more evidence he was unnatural. One time he'd pulled himself out for a guy—a human guy—and the guy had said, "That's a fucking monster." JT knew the guy hadn't meant anything bad by it, but he could already smell the fear on the guy (just a little bit, a notch or two above nervous) and so JT had spent the whole awful blowjob feeling just a bit shitty about himself.

He never felt shitty when Austin blew him. And unlike that other guy (and most people, to be honest), Austin had no trouble at all handling JT's size. Austin had cocksucking magic.

And it went like this:

He took JT's nuts in one hand and squeezed hard. JT liked his balls so sore they throbbed, and Austin knew it. JT went just a little dizzy from the wave of pain and let himself fall back against the minivan's side.

Austin spat on his cock a couple of times, got everything good and wet. Then cool lips closed over JT; then back teeth scraped gently. Austin took him all the way down while JT was still soft enough to make the tight warm bend where mouth became throat.

It was a wild thrill to see centimeter after centimeter of cock slide into Austin's mouth until there was nothing of it left to see, then to pull it out of him thinking the head would pop free any centimeter now, but it was just more and more veiny shaft. With Austin, he could enjoy the size of himself.

More exciting than the warm pain and tight slick throat—more exciting by far—was that JT could let himself go. JT, rarely a top, could let himself top when Austin blew him. He could pretend it was vengeance for all those times Austin was a dick to him: twenty-eight centimeters and two kilos of forest-green payback.

"Whaddya think of me now?" he grumbled, knowing the words meant nothing to Austin. He bat Austin upside the temple a couple of times, not fighting Austin's glamour, knowing this wasn't gonna last long enough for him to get too out of control.

He held Austin's head down on him with both hands. Austin could hold his breath for four minutes (they'd tried it to see). It only took three before JT was ready to blow.

Austin squeezed JT's nuts harder until JT saw stars. He struggled to get free of JT's huge pawlike hands. It was all fake, JT knew. Didn't matter it was fake, it still gave him the thrill he needed. Austin's squirming and all that warmth, that ache that wouldn't fade for an hour, and it was time. JT pulled himself out of Austin—ropes of thick spit splattering the concrete sidewalk, air suddenly cold on his dick—pulled himself out so just the tip of him was in Austin's mouth (still filling it), and he fired off.

JT let go of Austin's head, caught his breath, and checked the time. Four minutes, ten seconds. Not a record. "Happy now?"

Austin stood and wiped slop from his chin and flicked it to the ground. He grinned and nodded.

JT had expected some kind of wisecrack. Silence made him suspicious. "Swallow it."

Austin shook his head no and opened the door to the minivan.

"Austin, swallow it."

Austin ignored him and climbed in.

"Then spit it out," JT hissed after him.

Austin shot him a scandalized look. He wasn't the spitting kind.

JT followed him into the van. They pulled the door closed. Inside, hidden by the dark, JT glared at him and mouthed dire threats Austin pretended not to understand.

Ten minutes later it was time to roll. Austin and Grayson stepped out of the van together, checked each other's gear, and went off to rescue a dozen kids from an evil wizard's mad experiments. JT's last real-life view of Austin before it all went south: the elf let a thick glob of JT's come dribble from his mouth, then slurped it back in just to annoy him.

JT sat back, about to sink down into his drones' perception, and caught a glint of silver against the green of his hand. It was a strand of Austin's hair he'd pulled free—jet-black, reflecting the dash lights of the van. He held it and watched it curl. He dug his hand into his jeans and rearranged himself, already thickening again. And with Austin nowhere near, this time JT couldn't even blame it on the glamour.

CHAPTER TWO

The owner of the Victorian overlooking Buena Vista Park was on holiday in the Côte d'Azur. She had a really nice home. It was three stories, four if you counted the wine cellar, five if you counted the dragonfire shelter. When dragons had first appeared in the skies over Kuala Lumpur, San Francisco, London, and Paris, the terror they'd caused was 1962-one-minute-to-midnight. Dragonfire shelters became all the rage.

The Vic's kitchen was almost as beautiful as Duke Mason's kitchen. JT missed Duke Mason's kitchen. Every time he looked at the copper pots and pans here—not stored in cabinets, but hanging from a rack right over the kitchen workspace just like Duke's place—he wondered if he'd ever see Duke again. He missed Sunday-morning breakfast. Duke had loved having guests in his home, and he'd loved making Sunday breakfast.

He'd mix rice in Comet's scrambled eggs because he'd heard Chinese-Pacifickers did that. He would make JT a whole plateful of extra-crispy thick-sliced bacon, sometimes made from real pigs, and they said you couldn't tell the difference between that and the vat-grown but JT could because the vat-grown never had enough fat. And Duke would wear that apron that said *ORC CHEF* in beautiful cursive above a drawing of a cauldron with human limbs sticking out because he thought it was funny. Would Buzz ever see that apron? Because Buzz didn't have much sense of humor when it came to orcs and diet.

But them all sitting around the breakfast table at Duke's with the sun sparkling on the pool outside, big sliding doors all open, and a hot chlorine breeze blowing through, like they were all one big happy family, and Duke joyfully dirtying every pot and pan that hung from the ceiling—wouldn't that be nice?

Wasn't it strange the things that you focused on when someone was out of your life: not all the things about Duke that had pissed JT off (goddess, so many things), but Duke cooking breakfast?

Duke and Comet had been two of the first people JT had met after moving to Greentown, Arizona. It had been a sleazy kind of meeting: the best kind. And it was only after Comet and JT had fucked (and Duke had watched and coached them: "Put your hips into it, Comet!" "New Guy: beg him like you mean it! On your knees, tongue out! That's right! That's the way it's done.") . . . it was only after they'd fucked that JT found out who Duke was, and by then it had been too late.

Duke was the CEO of Irontooth Enterprises, one of the most influential private security companies on the globe. He was powerful, savvy, and violent—more like a Mafia don than a businessman—and he lived in a world only a half-step away from the criminal life JT had been trying to escape.

One thing had led to another: Duke had become an investor in JT's startup car factory, and JT hadn't been able to stay away from Comet—he'd had a crush one K deep back then—and so Duke became so much more than a business partner.

He was JT's patron. His financier. A role model. And there was something sexual there, sure, Duke, the voyeur daddy JT loved to please. Duke's praise gave JT a glow like few other things could. He'd have done anything for Duke (sometimes felt like he had), except tell him the truth about who he was.

Now Duke knew JT had lied to him. After Idaho, after Comet and Buzz had come to save him and had uncovered JT's false ID in the process, JT had confessed. He'd sent Duke a collection of files: flat-vid reports, and police and PBI files of unsolved crimes JT and Austin had committed over the years.

Then he'd cut off all communication with Duke, three-quarters guilt, one-quarter terror of what Duke would do. He imagined everything from blackmail, to shouting matches, to gunshots fired. Duke's messages piled up in JT's head, unopened, unread, unheard, unwatched.

And now here in this fucking kitchen of this fucking stolen home, all he could think about was how much he missed the Old Man, and not just Duke, but his old life where all he did was get drunk with Comet, let dirty soldier boys fuck him, and build cars with Dante.

Comet came in wearing Pacifica Army sweats and trainers.

"A bit late for you, isn't it?" It was 2 a.m. and Comet was a morning person.

Comet slid onto a barstool on the opposite side of the counter. "Can't sleep. Tried wearing myself out."

"Poor Buzz."

"Poor Buzz? He's happy and asleep. I thought I'd go jogging in the park."

"Stay. I'll make you some breakfast." He fetched a copper skillet from the ceiling rack and a package of bacon and carton of eggs from the Buick-sized fridge.

"Where'd you get eggs?"

"Grocery store?"

"You're a bunch of thieves."

"So I can't buy eggs?"

"What I mean is, shouldn't you be living off junk food and takeout?"

"Guess I got used to real food."

He cracked eggs and scrambled them in a bowl. He found a rice cooker, and that made Comet smile and shake his head. "You don't have to do that. I ain't never seen you cook before. You're thinking about Duke."

JT shrugged, not denying it. Comet was always like this, seeing right through JT. How JT had gotten away with lying to him for two years, he didn't know. He poured the eggs into the skillet, laid some bacon in another. Damn it. He'd done it all wrong—the eggs were supposed to be cooked in the bacon grease. That was how Duke did it. He almost poured the half-cooked eggs back in the mixing bowl, but you can't unscramble an egg.

Comet said, "I miss Duke. I can't sleep here. This house makes me nervous."

"You don't have to be here. Stay in a hotel. Hell, stay with your parents."

"Are you fucking crazy? Besides, they don't trust Buzz."

"You introduced Buzz to your parents?"

"Of course I did."

It seemed such a normal pedestrian thing to have done. And that made JT even more heartsick for Greentown. Never in his life had he met a boyfriend's parents. He dug a spatula under the eggs so they didn't burn. "And how did that go?"

"How do you think it went? He's a gold digger trying to steal their boy."

"You ain't got any gold."

"Far as they're concerned, I'm made of gold. I love them, but I ain't staying with my parents. I'm staying here with Buzz and with you, and I'm gonna help you because I'm your friend."

JT flipped the bacon, waited a few seconds, then flipped the strips again, afraid he'd burn them and mess up a simple breakfast.

Comet said, "It's not just squatting in this fucking house and sleeping in someone else's bed and using their TP and eating their food that's bothering me. It's you. I can't stand watching you do this. I don't like what I see."

Here it comes, JT thought. He'd lied to Comet about his real identity for two years, pretending to be a robotics and car engineer named Jason Taylor, when maybe (*maybe*) he hadn't needed to lie. That breach of trust was something he'd never repair. He deserved whatever rebuke Comet gave him. "I'm just making eggs." He pressed the bacon down with a spatula because that was what Duke did, and it sizzled. Then JT scraped it all onto a plate and slid it to Comet.

Comet said, "I ain't ever getting you back, am I?"

"You got Buzz." Shitty deflection number two, and Comet ignored it like he had the first one.

"You were my best friend, and I watch you here . . . I watch you planning the best way to kill people, I watch you analyze floorplans and guard rosters looking for weaknesses, and you know what? You're really good at it. And I think you enjoy it. And I don't want you to enjoy it. And I'm afraid you like it so much, you're gonna stay here— here in this fucking world filled with murderers and gangsters and thieves—and you're not gonna come back to us."

"I know it's a bad world. And I'm being very careful, Comet, okay? I got a fucking kid to worry about. I don't want Dante here, but she isn't gonna leave, you know that. And I have to make sure she stays alive so that she can go back with you to Greentown when this is all over. I'm being careful. I'm not getting sucked in."

He laid a fork down for him.

Comet said, "I want my friend back. Duke wants you back."

"You don't know that."

"Yes, I do."

"I asked you not to talk to him. I don't want him to know about any of this. I don't want to hear him try to argue me out of it. I don't want to hear him try to help. I asked you not to talk to him." Comet hadn't touched the fork. JT pushed it toward him.

Comet ignored it. "I haven't! I don't need to talk to him to know he wants you back. You've spent your whole life around shitty people, so you expect the worst even from the people who love you. I get that, but don't pretend it's fair or that we deserve it. Are you coming back to Greentown once this is over?"

"That's up to Duke now, isn't it?"

"Look, breakfast," Austin said coming in. "Do we have orange juice?"

Comet cocked his head, glanced at Austin, then back at JT and gave JT a humorless smile. "Oh, is that who it's up to? I think I'll take that jog after all." He pushed his plate away and shouldered past Austin.

Austin watched him leave. He sat in Comet's chair, took Comet's fork, examined it as if he could see germs, wiped it on his pants, nudged the bacon to the side, then dug into Comet's eggs. He shrugged. "More for me."

JT rolled his eyes. He wished Comet and Austin could get along, but the two of them were too similar in all the wrong ways, and he couldn't even imagine a world where they liked one another.

He busied himself with dishes and thought about his friends and the two worlds they came from and wished there was some way those worlds could overlap.

He thought of Dante and how he'd fucked up her life by being stupid enough to think he'd escaped his past and could have normal friends like normal people did, or mentor kids the way normal adults did, and maybe even save her life.

And what had that got her? A day in a coma that had to be cured by magic and had left her hurt. And what if she died on this job they were planning? Driving was the safest place for her. It was something she knew how to do. But plenty of drivers had been hurt or killed over the years and it was too damn easy to imagine her dead. When Valentine had attacked his compound and he and Austin had realized her target had been Dante, he'd panicked and frozen. It had been Austin who'd gotten to her first, Austin who'd fought Valentine off while JT pulled himself back to his senses and picked her up from the floor of the printer lab. Thinking she was dead, he'd wanted to die.

He couldn't do that again. He couldn't. There was only so much violence and death a person could stand.

He asked Austin, "When you were in Dante's head, what was it like?"

Austin stopped chewing his eggs and gave him a suspicious look. "What are you really asking?"

"I need your help."

"With what?"

"I'm going to tell Dante she's out."

THE JOB THAT WENT BAD
PART 2

When JT was young and running lookout for a ring of car thieves, the gang boss had kept JT in line with threats to sell him and stories of what buyers would do to him. Now as an adult, he still didn't know which of those stories were true and which ones weren't. Elf and orc kids disappeared all the time. The officials who studied such things said the numbers weren't reliable, no one really knew. They gave more excuses for doing nothing, but what they really meant was nobody cared. Elf kids in particular—especially elves of color (like Roan)—had become the favorite prey of child trafficking rings.

Their little gang's informants, a wide and only half-reliable network of gossips and bribed cops, had told them one of those rings was right here. The lab was an unobtrusive building on Hunter's Point, one of those shedlike light-industrial buildings. Inside were the kids they were going to save. For once, they'd be heroes.

JT fed Grayson and Austin constant chatter: —*Streets all clear for a block all directions. The lab's service door is locked.*

—*Camera override. Alarms disconnected*, Roan sent to JT, having patched into the lab by a splice in the city power grid. JT passed the news on to everyone. They'd long ago learned that multiple voices over coms just confused everyone, so it was JT's job to filter and pass on information: —*Opening service door. Three, two, one.*

Click.

Grayson and Austin hustled through.

JT watched through four different cameras: two street-side cameras mounted on drone fliers and one on each of the helmets Austin and Grayson wore. The images were strangely superimposed in JT's head. It made him feel like he was in five places at once.

The sensory feed would have made most people sick. To JT this was second nature. He felt free of his body, unconstrained, and there were times he wished he could stay like this forever.

His fifth sensor watched over Roan within the network. She skated over the facility's network and ambushed the virtual intelligences guarding critical systems. Their brief battles appeared as an uncanny Escherian scrolling, rotating, redrawings of the world. Roan was an artist. He loved to watch her work.

—*That was beautiful*, he sent to her after one particularly brilliant deletion of a bit of counterintrusion software they hadn't expected.

—*Thank you*, she sent. —*At least someone understands that I'm the backbone of this operation.*

Roan had been the backbone of everything. They had always known that.

Helmet cameras jittered and shook like they always did. It was past midnight and the lights were off except for emergency runners, and the light-gathering cameras showed everything in green. Both Austin and Grayson moved silent and slick as cats. Austin had three arrows in one hand and his bow in another. Grayson had an assault rifle. They watched for guards, watched for cameras their remote-controlled recon might have missed.

"Where are the guards?" Austin asked over his throat mic. And Austin was right, there should have been guards.

He saw Roan rescan the network, compare its topography to the visual feed from their helmets. —*Something's not right*, she said. She ran more scans.

—*Can I help?* JT asked, sending out of habit though they sat side by side.

—*Just watch my six.*

JT did, nervous because he wasn't the hacker, she was, and he was afraid he wouldn't know a threat when he saw one until it was too late.

Austin and Grayson turned a corner to a stairwell leading down. At the bottom, a basement hall would lead them into the dormitory where hijacked camera feeds had told them would be the kids they'd come to save.

—*Grayson, what's the ambient temp down there?* Roan asked. Grayson's armor had sensors for everything.

The dormitory was a long room. A dozen hospital beds lined both sides of a central aisle. The beds were bare, no sheets or blankets at all. No one slept in them.

—*Where's the kids?* Grayson sent. Both he and Austin stopped and scanned the room. But for the beds and a few wheeled tables, it was empty and had been for some time.

—*Temperature, Grayson?*

—*Eighteen degrees.*

People rarely thought about environmental sensors like light switches and thermostats as part of a building's network, but they were. The thermostats Roan was watching said twenty-two degrees Celsius, not eighteen. And even JT understood what that meant. The network Roan was in wasn't the building's actual network. It was the most elaborate virtual network simulation JT had ever seen. Precise even down to simulating inbound traffic that didn't actually exist, but not down to ambient temperature.

—*Shit.* Roan sent. —*Get out of there! Get out!*

The honeypot—usually a false database meant to entice thieves, this one here an entire false network—broke apart and revealed the true network behind it. It was filled with counterintrusion virtual intelligences. They looked like looming giants with sparkling teeth. Markers that JT recognized as turrets appeared in the topography. In the real world he saw the guns burst down from the dormitory's drop ceiling. Targeting lasers flashed through the dust.

JT flagged them for Grayson—Austin didn't have the tech to see the flagging and had to rely on preternatural senses. Through their cameras, JT saw Grayson shove Austin to the floor and out of the way. Then barrel flashes filled the room and everything went so noisy JT had to dampen the audio.

The force of the shots that hit Grayson drove him against the wall. His armor held, for a moment. Then he slid down with huge holes in him; huge holes in the wall behind him, light shining through his body like his soul leaking out. JT couldn't see Austin. Austin's camera was dark. Where was Austin?

JT called up identification and override software and attacked the turret's VI. The counterintrusion intelligences turned on him.

—*Out!* Roan sent. And suddenly JT was blinking, unable to process what his eyes saw. It took seconds for him to realize she'd kicked him from the network.

"No! No! Austin's still in there!" And his mind wrestled with the van's network to let him back in, make all the handshakes and security requests that he needed, but Roan had locked him out.

And then the horrible smell of burnt hair.

Blue flame danced atop Roan's head, and she shook violently in her harness.

Nothing made any sense after that. He held her on the van's floor and rocked her. He must have pulled her free of the harness, but didn't recall doing it. He might have opened the van door, didn't know. There were police lights, blue like the electrical fire that had shot through her, red like her blood. Outside, people shouted something cop-like; he didn't know what.

Holding her. Howling for Austin. Letting him know his sister was dead. Unable to imagine Austin dead too.

They tasered him. JT was an orc. It had taken four.

CHAPTER THREE

JT knocked at the door of the room Dante had claimed.
"It's three in the morning," Austin pointed out.

"She's a teenager."

Dante opened the door a crack.

"Can we talk?"

"It's three in the morning," she said.

"You're a teenager," he said.

She opened the door. She was wearing pajama bottoms and a sleeveless tee. There was something funny about an orc wearing pajamas. Dante had painted her toenails. He'd never noticed that before. They were burgundy, or whatever they called dark red these days. Her cane rested against the nightstand. It was druid crafted. JT had bought it for her: a shitty apology for ruining her life. Well, he wouldn't ruin it any more. She was going to go home.

She sat on the bed near the pillows. Austin stayed in the door, looking unwelcome and unhappy about agreeing to be there. JT sat near the foot of the bed.

He cleared his throat, trying to decide how to start this, but she said, "I couldn't sleep."

"Headaches?" The spell Austin had cast had brought her out of her coma, but hadn't been perfect. She had headaches, she tired easily, and when she got tired, her balance suffered. Hence the cane.

"Dreams."

She'd also had vivid dreams of the Blue Unicorn. The fragment of the RoanAI had taken up residence in her head. JT had thought the dreams had gone away when they'd played the AI's plea for help. He said so.

"They did. These are just normal dreams. Do you have any vids of her?"

"Vids?"

"She was your friend, wasn't she?"

Austin said, "JT has vids. I don't." Austin had no built-in tech. All his data—including vids of his sister—had been stored on a tablet that had been destroyed during the Job That Went Bad. JT had offered to copy the vids he had over. Austin had let him copy only a handful. As to the rest, he'd said, "Those are your memories, not mine."

JT picked a file at random from the store in his head and shared it with Dante.

In it: Roan is drunk as hell. She's hanging between Austin and Grayson, who lead her down the sidewalk. JT's recording, walking backward. She's shouting at passersby and giggling helplessly about who knows what. She sings songs at the top of her lungs. Roan is no singer.

She grabs Grayson by the collar and mumbles something in his ear. He says, "You ain't mine to lose," and it sounds like Grayson isn't happy, but Grayson wasn't ever happy, not that JT ever knew. She laughs like it is the funniest thing she ever heard—it's a rich laugh, but elegant the way people imagine elves must laugh—and Grayson smiles just a little bit and there's almost a hint of blush on his cheek.

"She couldn't hold wine for shit," JT said.

"She looks just like my dreams. How can I dream about someone I never met?" And JT realized that it wasn't just bad dreams going on. Dante seemed more upset than JT had ever seen her. She had spent nearly twenty-four hours in a coma. Medically speaking a coma and sleep were two very different states. For one: a comatose person didn't dream. But Austin said that Dante had dreamt. And though he wouldn't share the specifics of those dreams ("Those aren't my stories to tell," he said, which had been uncharacteristically respectful for Austin) Roan had been present in them, haunting Dante like a ghost.

"What was she like?" she said.

Now he'd been asked, JT didn't know what to say. How did you describe a person in just a few words and not make her sound like every other?

Austin answered for him. "She was stubborn and brilliant, and she was always afraid she was wrong even when she wasn't. She hated being afraid. She hated that I could tell when she was, so I always had to hide it." He looked away and shuffled his feet and hesitantly said, "She was like you, a little."

JT expected Dante to snap at him because the two of them had gotten off to a bad start (everyone got off to a bad start with Austin, it seemed), and things had only gone downhill since. That comment had been the kind of presumptuous thing that would make Dante snap.

She didn't. She gave him a narrow-eyed glare, her eyes going candle-light, showing she was worked up, like she was scanning him for bullshit. But Austin wasn't shitting.

Dante almost smiled. "When we rescue her, I'll finally meet her."

"It's not her," Austin said. "Roan's dead."

Dante didn't seem to hear him. "It's gonna be fucking weird as hell, ya know? She won't know me, but I'll know her. And she'll know you guys, but you won't know her. What are you all going to do once you're together again?"

"It's not her. Roan's dead," Austin said again. "We can't ever be together."

"Sure you can," she said.

JT's skin crawled. He wanted to tell her, *Shut up, can't you see you're upsetting him.* But JT had wondered too. When it was the three of them again, what would they do? He had this dream he barely acknowledged: Roan reborn, bodiless, electronic, and perfect. Maybe she'd teach JT how she did it, and then he'd do the same and he wouldn't be an orc anymore. He'd be a ghost in the machine, same as her. Then he could be anything he wanted.

"I can't access tech," Austin said.

"You'd do it if it gave you your sister back," Dante said.

"My sister is gone. I won't make the same sacrifices she did just so I can have the illusion of her being alive. I said she wasn't wrong very often. She was wrong when she turned away from magic to spite our grandfather. I wish I'd told her that before she died."

He said all these things far more calmly than JT would have ever imagined. For JT, Roan's death was a raw wound he'd avoided for two years. He'd thought Austin's obsessions would have made him the same, but Austin wasn't the same.

Dante said, "Still, I want to meet her. So what's going on? Why are you here?"

JT said, "Dante, I don't think—"

"I got a job for you," Austin said.

"A job?" Dante brightened and seemed to forget she didn't like Austin.

"There's a guy I want you to recruit. An elf. He won't like us. He *will* like you."

Goddess, look at her fucking glow.

"That wasn't what we went in there for!" JT hissed at Austin in the hall. "That was the exact opposite of what we went in there for!"

"She's as much a part of this as anyone, JT, and it isn't your call or mine as to whether she's part of the team. The RoanAI made that call when she created the Blue Unicorn and sent it after Dante."

Austin's sense of fatalism was annoying as hell.

"I'm going to bed," Austin said and left JT there, tired and sleepless.

The dining room table could have sat a football team. In the center of the table was a fruit bowl. JT had filled it with fruit. Tucked amid the fruit was a unicorn horn rusted with the dried blood of a wizard. That had been Austin's contribution to the décor. No one ate the fruit. Next to the bowl lay a hockey puck-shaped holo-projector. Like all holo-projectors, it worked by filling the air above it with a cloud of nano-particles set to fluoresce programmatically. It was monochrome green (full-color holo-projection still looked like mud) and high-end, which meant the fluorescent cloud didn't scatter and blur the image. Dead particles dusted the table. JT wiped them away every day.

JT and Buzz were networked to this projector 24/7. It contained what they all called the Death Star Plans, on account of the joke the Blue Unicorn had told when it had hidden the plans in Dante's subconscious: "Help me, Dante Riggs. You're my only hope."

A 3-D map of Alcatraz Island rotated above the puck.

The prison house and its adjoining administration facilities were wrecks. Public funding for the island had diminished as the Bay Area had enclaved and its tax base fallen through the floor. The privatization of the island had been unpopular. First People, Druids, and preservationist organizations fought it. By the time The Thousand Suns purchased the island, the building—always doomed to a salty demise—was well on its way to collapsing. Firelight had fused his tower into the rusting hulk of the prison. He'd done it overnight.

Some said he'd called out spirits from the jailhouse—ghosts of the eight men who'd been murdered there when it was a prison—and set them to work. Other people claimed other things—blood sacrifice to chthonic powers, an army of elemental gnomes or demons, the CTexas government, Russians, or aliens—but the fact was: one day the castle wasn't there and the next day it was, Neuschwanstein meets Castlevania superimposed over the prison like two (or three) realities had merged, part concrete and steel, part stone. And the highest tower of the castle—Firelight's Tower—rose a good fifty meters higher than the old prison lighthouse, and the flames within it did a much better job at warning people away. It stood nowhere near as tall as the Sorcerer's Tower that had replaced the old Transamerica Pyramid on the peninsula. But where the Sorcerer's Tower promised magical blessings on the people who lived in its shadow, this tower promised curses.

The Death Star Plans weren't just floor plans. There were electrical and HVAC overlays. Network overlays. There were membership rosters for The Thousand Suns and all the staff it took to run the place. There were guard rotations. And there was one overlay that none of them knew quite how to interpret; it was filled with magical symbols. Austin's training was druidic in nature, and while he could guess those symbols there in the Bay marked the dens of enslaved water spirits, most of the symbols meant nothing to him. They needed a wizard.

In the lowest level of the complex, amid newly dug chambers below even the Spanish Dungeon lay a TEMPEST-hardened room, a high-security, network-dead room meant for storing sensitive data—or imprisoning an AI. But the only truly secure data was data never accessed, and the RoanAI had been accessed many times. Over two years, she had managed to collect the plans and charts and schedules floating here in green. She'd released countless "ghost" fragments to search for JT and Austin, one of which—the Blue Unicorn—had finally delivered the plans to them through Dante.

The data was incomplete. Parts of the maps (particularly those of the castle) were blank. But it was enough for a prison break.

JT swept his hand through the 3-D image. The nano-particles were too small to feel, no more than you could feel a ghost. The image swirled, then stabilized.

His hand fell to the puck itself, and he laid his fingers softly on it.

—*Roan, are you in there?*

Sometimes the Blue Unicorn looked like a unicorn with a bluish coat. Other times it looked like Roan herself: an African American elf, lithe, frizzy hair, surrounded by butterflies. The Unicorn had been an odd collection of memories from Roan's childhood: memories of finding a blue unicorn in the forests of Washington state, of Roan's surgery when she'd gotten her implants, of her and Austin harassed by a mounted police officer in Seattle because they were young and she was black. And though JT knew that the Blue Unicorn wasn't Roan (wasn't even technically the RoanAI, only a shed part of it, an agent) it was hard not to think it was her in some way.

Contrary to all known science, the Blue Unicorn projected Roan's glamour. Computers couldn't have glamours, everyone knew that. Computers couldn't cast spells. And that was what had started this all: The Electric Dragon Triad had caught the Blue Unicorn, felt her glamour, and had hired Buzz to replicate it to use in pornography. They'd been laughably short-sighted. A computer program with a glamour meant so much more than money. It hinted at the unification of magic and science.

Roan's glamour (the Blue Unicorn's glamour) was a bittersweet sensual melancholy. And that glamour, that sense of sweet loss, made it harder to accept that the Blue Unicorn wasn't really Roan.

—Roan, are you in there?

Whenever he sat here and watched the island spin lazily over the table, he thought he felt her. But maybe it was nothing but the usual kind of grief one had. That was the problem with glamour: real became unreal and vice versa. It was why he'd never been sure he could trust his feelings about Austin. What orc in his right mind thought he could win the love of an elf like him? Austin, who had always been crazy, inconstant, inconsiderate, a whole bunch of other in- words, and didn't that prove that it was only his glamour JT felt when he saw Austin smile, and not something deeper?

Goddess, how he missed her. She'd always been the sensible one. JT sat there next to the projector and its green Death Star Plans and tried to sort his feelings into real and unreal, all the while calling her name.

THE JOB THAT WENT BAD
PART 3

When his taser-and-drug-induced daze finally cleared, JT knew something was wrong.

Those cops who had tasered him—either they hadn't been cops at all, or they'd been corrupt and had sold him off to whoever was paying. He knew this because he wasn't in jail, at least not any jail he'd ever seen. The room was jail-cell-*like*, sure: One wall consisted of bars and a gate. Another had bolted-in manacles, two at the top, and two at the bottom. They looked medieval, except that the manacles were padded with leather. Somehow that made the threat of them worse, like whatever his captors were planning to do, they needed to take a bit of care or else he would break.

The light in the cell was dim and comfortable. He heard footsteps outside but through the bars he saw no one, just an antiseptic hall, hospital-like.

"Austin!" he shouted, not *Roan*. (And later he felt a bit guilty for that because he should have called for her.) But there was no response, and even if there had been, his panicked heartbeat would have covered the sound.

He closed his eyes and calmed himself. He felt for Austin's glamour. For one hopeful moment, he thought he felt them both: a hint of Austin's aggressive lust, *and* Roan's melancholy.

No. This sorrow—deep and focused, painful and terrible—wasn't Roan's glamour. It wasn't romantic sentiment, but true grief. He'd seen her die.

But this vague arousal that set him on edge, *that* was Austin's glamour. It was weak and distant like the old memory of a good hard fuck. Austin's glamour, no mistaking. Austin was alive, and he was nearby. It felt stronger near the wall with the manacles. JT beat on it and shouted his name, but there was still no response.

Hours later, burly guards came in and tried to chain him to the wall. He fought, but they overwhelmed him and beat him. Finally, a wizard's acolyte (he could tell by the robes) scolded them all for bruising "the subject." They backed off and left him alone, and JT was stupid enough to think he had won.

Then Firelight entered the room.

Wizards were terrifying. Worse than orcs. Flames licked over Firelight, along the creases of his black robes, over his hands and neck and face, and devoured him. He smelled like burnt dinner, and it made JT's mouth water and that made his stomach flip.

"I am Firelight Who Had Stood in the Maw of Abbadon the Red, Was Consumed and Reborn, Archmagus of the Thousand Suns." There was something about the casual tone by which the wizard spoke of his own death that made the ostentatious name unmockable. "And you are JT. No last name. No title at all. But nevertheless a very special orc. Together, you and I will unlock the secret of magic."

JT frowned; that didn't seem likely. "What do I know about magic?"

"Nothing. But orcs are hypersensitive to glamours, and you more than most. Future acolytes will learn your name. You'll be a hero."

"I don't want to be a hero."

"No sane person does. Now . . . you can fight my guards and researchers, or you can cooperate. The end result will be the same, except for the pain involved."

JT glared at the guards. They glared back. He wasn't afraid of them. Firelight, however . . . He watched Firelight burn and could see the wizard's pain. It was all too easy to imagine the wizard setting JT on fire too, so he allowed himself to be chained to the wall.

Acolytes and techs busied themselves. It was confusing as hell. Techs snapped a jack into his skull and wheeled in a computer on a little stand and started calibrating what, JT didn't know. Under Firelight's supervision, the acolytes took small dishes of paint and finger painted the walls around JT with blood-colored symbols that made JT's skin crawl. The paint burned for a moment and then went out.

When they finished the design, they left and the techs took measurements of JT's mind, recording his sensations like he was a sim-flick actor. It was the modern medical version of "tell me if this hurts," except they didn't have to ask, they could just review the sensations themselves.

It was all terrifying, but it didn't hurt and JT (being JT) became curious as to what exactly they hoped to achieve. He asked a lot of questions. They didn't answer any of them. When their tests for that day were over, they unchained him, and it felt like a whole lot of ado over nothing.

At night the paint faded away.

The next day they did it again. It reminded him of when he'd been a kid and of the lab that had birthed him and how they never had treated him badly except for the fact he'd been a prisoner. He told Firelight and the techs he'd cooperate if they only told him what it was they were doing. They ignored him.

He told himself he was no longer that little orc boy needing attention and only getting it when he did what the scientists asked. He was an adult now and wise enough to know it didn't matter how well they treated him. He was a prisoner. They'd taken his freedom for their experiments, and it didn't matter if those experiments caused him pain or not, or what they were for. He'd have killed every last one of them to be free.

One day, they drew a certain pattern, different than all the ones before, and a warmth passed through him. It ran straight from his heart to the base of his cock, and he started to go hard. The lab techs talked fast with each other (all in some language JT didn't know) and pointed at the screens. Then they pointed to the growing bulge in the crotch of the cheap hospital scrubs they'd given him to wear.

It was Austin's glamour that he felt, and it wasn't distant and nagging like it had been for weeks, but strong—so strong he was sure Austin stood just outside, right there just outside the door around the corner where no one could see. Austin was coming to save him! JT knew it!

"Austin! Austin!" he bellowed and let the elf's glamour—that part that had always put him on edge and made him want to fight—he let the elf's glamour take him. He focused it into a rage against the wizards and techs. He fought against the chains. "Austin! I'm here!"

Firelight grinned wide, and the flames that continually devoured his body ran across his jaw. His lips curled even further, smile maniacal, until they fell away in ash. He took a cloth and wiped the drawings from the wall.

Immediately, Austin's glamour dimmed to nearly nothing. And JT understood vaguely, heartbreakingly, that Austin had never been outside the door. It had only been the wizard's magic.

"No! No, bring him back! Bring him back! Draw them again!" Because even the illusion of Austin was better than nothing.

But they took their equipment and turned out the lights. The manacles dropped from his ankles and wrists. He collapsed to the floor and spent a long time in the darkness alone. He pawed at the wall where he'd hung and begged for his friend, but though he could sense him, it was as though Austin was far away and couldn't come closer.

Days of this passed.

Sometimes when they drew their diagrams, nothing would happen and Austin's glamour would remain a distant flicker of desire. Other times, JT would feel Austin's glamour so strongly he'd have sworn the elf was standing right beside him, even touching him. He'd close his eyes, and Austin would appear: shirtless with scars everywhere, naked cock proud, and JT would beg Austin to fuck him. He'd whisper it so that the wizard and his acolytes couldn't hear. But their monitors were jacked directly into him and their machines holo-projected whatever he thought or imagined into the room. JT could keep no secrets from them.

And despite the humiliation of it all, he welcomed Austin's glamour. Wasn't it ironic? JT had spent four years fighting Austin's glamour, but now here he welcomed it and wished it was Austin in the flesh.

At night he crawled to the wall (always cleaned of symbols) and spoke aloud like the afterglow of Firelight's magic could translate his words across space and time.

"Austin, can you hear me?"

There alone in the darkness, in a room nothing like a Catholic confessional, he confessed everything. He told Austin how he'd fallen in love with him at first sight, how he'd been too afraid of rejection to act on it, how he resented Austin for being an elf and so beautiful.

"I've always been afraid of your glamour. I've always been afraid of how amazing you are. When I'm around you, I feel . . . out of control. The guys you'd bring home—all these beautiful guys—they'd all fall in love too, and as soon as they did, you'd lose interest and dump them.

"I'm an orc and a monster. People are afraid of me. What did I have those other guys didn't have? I didn't have nothing.

"The only way I could be with you was to not fall in love. So I tried. I tried really hard, but it didn't work. Because you'd give me that look that you do, and the next thing I knew we'd be fucking. And I told myself it was your glamour and not that I wanted you."

And now, when all he had was Austin's glamour, he knew what he wanted was Austin himself.

He knew that Austin couldn't hear him. That was good because he'd have said none of this if Austin could have heard. (But what if Austin could hear and JT wouldn't have to go through the shame of admitting it all, face-to-face?)

He banged his forehead against the wall in frustration. *Crack. Crack. Crack.* The pain clarified him for a moment.

Something knocked back, dimly, softly, almost a mirage.

"Austin?"

He knocked hard on the wall with his knuckles.

Three knocks back.

This was no wizard's magic: it was Austin right there on the other side of the wall, the way JT had always known.

The next day they switched up the symbols again, and this time the sense of Austin was so perfectly re-created and reinforced by the knowledge that Austin was right there on the other side of the very wall he was chained to—that JT came.

And as he did, the lights in the room flickered and went out and the walls were replaced by darkness, and in the darkness stars appeared in strange constellations. The techs and acolytes panicked and stumbled over each other to escape the room, and then all that was left there was Firelight and himself suspended in space.

Firelight turned slowly, examining the darkness and its constellations. He said, "This is a vision you're having, isn't it, made manifest by the holo-projector? Where do these come from? Do you always have such hallucinations when you're aroused? Or is it just Austin that—"

JT roared, nearly mindless with rage. He yanked and strained against the manacles, and they rattled and clanked but didn't break.

Firelight showed no alarm at all. "Look at you, barely more than a beast. No words, no language at all. Is this what the elf makes of you? And what if I were to . . ." And he swiped his hand over the wall, smearing the complicated patterns his acolytes had drawn there.

JT gasped as Austin's glamour fled him instantly, leaving an overwhelming absence. All his rage and lust disappeared. His cock softened. The manacles came undone, and he fell to the floor. Firelight didn't try to catch him. JT crawled to the cell bed—nothing more than a metal cot—and pulled its one blanket over him to hide his humiliation and shame.

"Interesting," Firelight said. "I wonder what visions you'll share tomorrow."

JT said, "I will kill you. Austin and I will kill you."

Firelight held out his hand as if he was going to touch JT. It should have been an elegant hand, the hand of a concert pianist, but his curse had ruined it. Tiny flames passed over his hand in waves. His skin reddened and blistered. And after they passed, his skin healed as if nothing had happened, but his hand still trembled softly as if it remembered the pain. Then the flames returned, larger and brighter until they engulfed the hand completely as hot and fierce as magnesium, and JT had to close his eyes. Charred pieces of the wizard pattered to the floor, sounding like rain, and the room filled with the stink.

The glow through his eyelids died, and he opened his eyes. There was nothing left of the wizard's hand but blackened bone, and then—just like that—the hand was restored. "I am immortal. You and Austin, however . . . I will use you up. I will learn everything I can from your bodies, and then when you're as empty as a take-out carton, I will incinerate you like the trash you've always been."

At night JT confessed his soul to Austin behind the wall. During the day, Firelight and his disciples ran their experiments, leaving him exhausted and humiliated. Until one day:

The lights died everywhere and the emergency lights came on. Sirens blared in the halls. A recorded voice said, "This is not a test." JT's first thought was The Bomb or Dragonfire, he'd lived under those threats so long. He'd be incinerated any moment. It was the kind of instant and inevitable death his generation had been trained to expect: Ragnarok—what could you do?

The door sprang open. He expected the guards and techs as usual, but no one came in, so he took his single blanket and went out. Red emergency lights lit the hall from the floor. He saw no one at first.

"JT?" came Austin's voice from behind him.

He turned, and there was Austin stepping out of the cell adjacent to his.

They rushed together and fell into each other's arms. JT kissed him. He held him tight and kissed him, but they were orc kisses and it was all jabbing tusks and JT running his tongue sloppily over him. And he felt Austin's glamour entwine his soul and he didn't fight it at all, and his eyes filled with sparks that splattered from Austin's shoulder when they fell. They stood in the middle of the hall, sirens blaring and the two of them giggling like madmen refusing to let go, and maybe JT was. Maybe the wizards had finally broken him.

Austin pulled away. He had to fight JT to be free of him. "What the hell's wrong with you? What's wrong, JT?"

"Roan's dead."

"No. No, I feel her glamour."

It had never occurred to JT until now that an elf could be confused between what was real and what was glamour, the way other species were. He had spent four years in vicious self-debate over whether what he felt for Austin was real love or only the sexual urgings of Austin's glamour. He'd spent four years debating whether he was simply introspective and morose by nature or those thoughts had been caused by Roan. Those two internal wrestling matches had torn him, and knotted him up, and bewildered him, until that moment by the wall when everything had become clear and he'd confessed.

Here was Austin caught in the same torn, knotted confusion. The trick that Austin's mind was playing on itself was perfectly plain to JT because he had done the same thing. In Austin's need for his sister to have survived, Austin was mistaking the reality of his grief for the fiction of her glamour.

"I'm sorry, Austin. I saw her die."

Austin looked around dazedly, and finally the chaos around them seemed to register. "We should run."

They ran hand in hand because neither would let go of the other. They passed shot-up guards and techs. The walls were blasted like there'd been a fight. The barrels of turrets suspended from the ceiling smoked. They found a stairwell and went up. They listened at a door and heard distant shouting and gunfire. They ran the other way.

They burst from a service door out into a San Francisco street not six blocks from the Hunter's Point lab where they'd been captured, and they escaped.

CHAPTER FOUR

Dante tired easily and it pissed her off. Buzz had told her it was residual damage from her brief time in a coma and she'd heal, but he wasn't a doctor, so what the fuck did he know?

She didn't like the way everyone treated her, especially Austin. Austin looked away from her when she had to hold a counter for balance or lean against a wall while she took a deep breath, like it was his fault her body wasn't working so well. She wanted to tell him it wasn't. It was because of him she was moving at all, but pride kept her from saying that. She knew it was pride, and she knew she was wrong, but she wasn't ready to admit that yet. That pissed her off too. It made her feel petty.

JT had bought her a cane. That had pissed her off until she'd seen it. It was druid-crafted by the kind of druids that hung out in Golden Gate Park and grew their own smokes (*caveat emptor*). It was two kinds of wood, one light and one dark, twisted together, and the dark one bloomed into a demon's head. It was king-of-fucks cool.

Even so, it took her forever to get to the stupid antique store, and by the time she got there she was exhausted.

Until she saw him again.

Nicolás Ruiz-Chavez was all of sixteen (a year younger than her), jeans sinfully tight, black, and razor-ripped. His antique biker's jacket studded and chained, *La Calavera Catrina* on the back, brilliantly colored. His black hair was cut jagged. His long sharp ears were pierced nine times: ring after ring. His nose was studded, lower lip just the once, one eyebrow in a row of tiny steel loops, the other shaved in Morse code: SOS.

He smelled like something she couldn't quite place. Not a perfume.

Nico stood in the center of the store, casually shopping.

"What the fuck you looking at?" he said, tiny flash of a tongue piercing. She tried not to imagine how that would feel against her clit, but failed.

"What is this place?" Dante said. They'd never spoken before, and she was nervous.

He glanced to the front window of the store. The word *VINYL* was painted across it.

"It's an antique store. These are records." He pulled a square of cardboard from its bamboo crate and waved it in the air. His voice dripped sarcasm. Dante didn't react to his bullshit. She knew what "records" were, vaguely. She'd never seen one before. He said, "It's music stamped on vinyl disks. You need special equipment to hear them. It sounds like crap."

There was a whole store filled with them. "Why would you want one?"

"To be pretentious." He shrugged. "Or authentic."

There had to be a word that meant more than beautiful. Angelic. Angelic and angry and perfectly damaged, and she knew half of what her senses told her about him was a lie. What of him was glamour and what of him was him? Was the polish on his nails really that shade of purple? Lips matching red? Did his hair always fall in his eyes, or just now? Did JT see Austin this way? If so, was it any wonder JT was a fuckin' basket case around the elf?

She should go. This was a bad idea, and Austin had been wrong to think she could pull it off. Instead she said, "So: pretentious or authentic? Which one are you?" It was such an orc thing to do: respond to insecurity with an attack.

He smiled (perfectly) and tapped his tongue piercing against his teeth. "You were the one staring. You tell me."

"I wasn't—" She gave up and shrugged. "Thousands of people look just like you do. Put a safety pin through your eyebrow, you'd be a hundred years retro."

"So your vote is pretentious."

"I don't think you can help it. That makes it authentic."

His smile went lopsided, unconvinced by Dante's logic.

Dante broke eye contact (both hard and a crazy relief) and flipped through cardboard sleeves like she cared, and said like she didn't care: "You've been casing this place for a week now. I've been watching. I know who you are. Nicolás Ruiz-Chavez. NRC. Your tag is all over City Netspace. It's on Godzilla's tail, the underside where hardly anyone sees."

She waited for the elf to run. Dante would have run in his place. Nico didn't.

"Godzilla was there before I was born."

"You didn't build him, you tagged him. And no one erased it. No one reset him. That means someone respects you."

"You ain't a cop. What do you want?"

"I want in." JT and Austin had told her she'd have to prove herself, and this seemed as good a way as any.

"In on what?"

"Whatever you're doing here."

"Ain't nothing I'm doing."

"Bullshit. Let me in."

"Fine. You know so much, then get in position. And if you fuck this up, I'll put a bullet in you. Don't think I won't."

Bullshit. This guy wouldn't shoot a fly. Dante almost asked questions. She almost asked for them to link up so they could talk net-wise, but this was part of the test. Any questions, any chatter at all, and Dante would lose face.

VINYL was a long, narrow shop. The floorplan was simple. Against the walls were tables stacked with bamboo crates filled with the cardboard sleeves of antique records. In the center stood a long island of more crates.

On the left wall of the place ran an elaborate illusion. City Netspace was an augmented reality, a virtual overlay that covered much of the Bay Area. It was the playground of artists and street gangs. JT had first showed it to her at Lombard Street. She'd seen a virtual school of fish swim down the twisted road. It had been followed by a school of sperm. Since then, Dante had the Netspace running 24/7. Here on VINYL's interior wall, the Netspace showed performances of long-dead musicians positioned as if VINYL was a shop hanging in the air at the rear of a stadium. It was disorienting and gave Dante vertigo.

Over the past week she'd lurked around the place, watching and recording, and Buzz had taken her recordings and run them through the data-mining processes normally only used by governments trying to uncover terrorist cells. It searched the timing of Nico's visits to the store and the visits, calls, and custom of everyone else, looking for patterns and commonalities. Buzz's analysis had suggested (with a very strong reliability) that Nico was tracking a customer named Nchede Comorra. Comorra had ordered an exceptionally rare vinyl copy of Funkadelic's *Maggot Brain*. It had arrived yesterday. Nico was here today to steal it.

And, right on time, Comorra walked through the door.

Dante didn't know how Nico planned to pull this off. For a shop that sold useless musical recordings, there were a lot of fucking people in here, and as one of the last un-enclaved neighborhoods in SF, the sidewalks of Haight-Ashbury were always busy.

She checked the back door. There were cameras there. She signaled Buzz. She went near the door and pretended to shop, flipping through album after album. She'd never heard of any of this music before. This was all JT kind of shit. Music by dead people.

From the corner of her eye, she watched Comorra walk to the kiosk, tap her fingers against its screen. It read her prints, transferred money, and politely asked her to wait while her purchase was brought out.

One minute later a wall to the stockroom/safe slid open and an airborne drone hummed out, a square thin package in its grip.

Comorra said, "About fucking time."

Nico smiled and mouthed to Dante, *I agree.*

All hell broke loose. Tentacles erupted from the walls. They thrashed and coiled and their suckers pulsed and every damn person in that place screeched in terror and fell to the ground. Some fucking bastard pulled a gun and started shooting at ghosts. The sudden scent of fear that filled the place went straight to Dante's head, almost as strong as Nico's glamour, making her dizzy with the need to attack. She fought it and cowered near the door, confused.

Except this was it, wasn't it? This was the whole plan after all:

Nico Ruiz-Chavez was a City Netspace artist. Everyone in this store with Netspace access would login to watch the illusionary concerts. Those tentacles were Nico's hack of the local City Netspace, meant to scare the shit out of everyone (which they did), and give him the moment he needed (which it did).

She signaled Buzz. He cut the cameras.

Nico snatched the package from the drone and slipped past Dante through the door into the alley. Some stalwart citizen—the fucking bastard with the gun—tried to chase him. Dante played panicked orc, got in his way and bowled him over. He went sprawling, cursing, his pistol clattering away beneath crates, and he tore them apart to recover his weapon.

Dante ducked out the back door. It was dark, foggy. Suddenly tired, she limped her way down the alley. Her cane clacked. She didn't see Nico. She sighed. She should have known this would happen. Had it been her, she'd have done the same thing.

Behind her: "You followed me for a week. What's your game?"

She turned and there was Nico, holding a pistol on her. Tucked beneath his arm was the Funkadelic album, unwrapped. Its cover was a screaming woman of African descent buried to her neck in dirt. The image was horrifying. Why would anyone want something like that?

His gun was very steady. Maybe he'd shoot her after all.

"How long are those tentacles gonna infest the place?"

"Until they figure out how to wipe them."

"I need you for a job."

"A job."

"A prison break. Sort of."

"You're shitting me. I don't do prison breaks. I'm strictly small-time. Prison break of who? What do you need me for?"

"Special weapon," she said because that was what Austin had called him and she knew Nico would like the sound of that. She added, "What's my take?"

"Your what?"

"I helped you steal your stupid antique. You owe me money. What's my take?"

Nico slipped his pistol into an inside pocket of his leather jacket. He gave her the most wickedly beautiful smile she'd ever seen, all ornery sweetness she knew she couldn't trust. He held up the album so she could see its cover by the distant alleyway lights. "I'll let you listen to my new record."

"Fuck that." She wasn't so naive as that. No one was so naive as that, except maybe JT. She wasn't gonna fall for this guy like JT fell for Austin. She was smarter than that.

Later, in a darkened room, cannabis mixing with his mysterious scent, she sat as far from him as possible, and he didn't laugh at her but seemed a little sad when she told him why. His glamour felt like a stolen car: illicit, powerful, not hers but something she could take if she wanted, not by brute force but by skill and daring and smarts. Between them, the vinyl spun slowly at 33 1/3 RPMs and hissed and scratched and popped, more noise than music, and she didn't even care. Resisting him was a high like she'd never known.

Dante had complained that the Japanese Tea Garden would make the meeting feel like a date.

Austin said, "Is it?"

"Fuck you, I ain't dumb enough to date a fucking elf."

Austin had rolled his eyes. "Yeah, that's what everyone says."

They'd asked Dante not to tell Nico who he was meeting. Dante hadn't liked that. Nico didn't either. He went suspicious right away, and she thought it was only the location that made him say yes.

JT and Austin were sitting on one of the rungs of the high-arched Drum Bridge, beer bottles in hand and a cooler on the ground nearby, looking more like college-boy trespassers than mastermind criminals. That had been intentional too.

None of it worked. "Son of a fuck. I'm outta here," Nico said as soon as he saw who he was meeting.

She grabbed his arm. "Nico, wait."

"If you had any sense, you'd be out of here too."

"Look, I don't know what you heard—"

"What I heard? What I heard is that Lisa Kuang-Li and the Electric Dragon Triad are after these two, and they ain't gonna think twice about cutting down some elf boy who happens to be standing too close. I should have known better than to listen to you. You're gonna get yourself killed. They're gonna get you killed." He pulled his arm free and stalked off up the narrow sidewalk muttering curses to himself.

"Fine!" she shouted after him. "Fine, just spend the rest of your life stealing plastic antiques."

He rounded, but kept walking backward away from her. "I steal other things too. Antiques are easy, hard to trace, and keep me eating. And no one wants to kill me!"

"If all you wanted was easy money, you wouldn't have tagged Godzilla's fucking tail!"

Nico didn't stop. He turned the corner and disappeared into the Garden.

"Fuck!" Dante said and smacked the pavement with her cane. She stalked back to JT, dreading the look of disappointment on his face. She sent, —*I'm sorry. I fucked it up.*

JT didn't look disappointed. He popped a beer open with his tusk and spat the cap into the little cooler. He gave it to her. He popped another one and held it out too. She didn't need two beers and was gonna say so, but he wasn't offering it to her.

Coming up behind her quiet as a cat—quiet as any elf could be—Nico took the beer. "You got till I'm done with this beer to tell me how famous I'm gonna be."

THE JOB THAT WENT BAD
PART 4

JT and Austin fled to the public-access portion of Pacific Heights and in the alley between two ancient five-story homes they found a stairway to a basement no one had visited in fifty years or more. JT broke the lock, and inside it smelled like mold and mildew so badly any other time he'd have worried for their health.

They took the corner farthest from the stairwell and built it into a redoubt. They stole clothes and food and blankets. Orc and elf, they didn't need lamps for light.

They huddled there and watched the door. For three days they ate out of tins. They pissed and shat in the corner, no toilet, one guarding the other, eyes on the door.

They held each other.

They didn't talk much, except: "It will be okay."

"I know."

And sometimes it was JT who said it, sometimes it was Austin. They didn't talk about Roan or what had happened while they'd been prisoners.

They watched the door.

Elves could see in dim light, but orcs could see in the dark. Orcs were creatures of darkness. For most, darkness meant terror. For orcs, darkness meant they could finally see the beauty no one else understood. People thought orc eyes saw beyond the human-visible spectrum into infrared or ultraviolet, or that they were somehow light-gathering like night goggles were. But JT had worn infrared and light-gathering goggles before; they weren't the same. To JT, darkness was a many-textured thing obscured by the visible spectrum, and it was only when that interference was gone—all the lights turned out—that the world shone in all its beauty.

There was nothing in the world more beautiful than Austin in the pitch-black of that Pacific Heights cellar. He was wholly his glamour, no muscles, no scars, only a shifting sequence of moods. Austin's revealed soul: shockingly gentle, unsurprisingly sharp. In the darkness, Austin was pulsar-bright.

They'd hold each other (JT's back against the wall and his arms around the sun that was Austin), and they'd watch the door, and JT would forget to be afraid.

"Make love to me," he said.

They never talked like that. Never *make love*. They made fun of people who said things like that.

JT would undo his stolen jeans and slide them down, and Austin would take JT's heavy legs in the crook of his arms and fold them back and try his best to make love. Or Austin would hold him—wiry arms around JT's chest, fingertips stroking, following the runnels between muscle that JT still had back then. Austin would kiss him—hot lips against his neck, sucking at the tips of JT's pointed ears. Sucking hardened nipples. And Austin's cock would slide gently in and out of him like a prayer.

JT was the happiest he'd ever been. He had Austin again, and they shared something they'd never shared before, here in the worst of places at the worst of times.

It lasted until the guilt crept up on him, until the sudden movement of some rat in the corner, some siren outside, would snap him out of his dream and he'd remember that the wizards would find them and imprison them again. He'd remember Roan and Grayson were dead. And he'd think, *What kind of selfish shit am I to find happiness now? What kind of inhuman trash? What kind of monster would fall in love now?* Because that's what he was doing—falling in love.

No, he'd always been in love. But he was reaching a place where he couldn't deny it.

He'd push Austin away from him, and Austin would let go slowly and wouldn't complain, but say, "Whatever you need."

And then, later, at night when everything felt hopeless again and JT's mood ebbed lowest and he felt ready to break, he'd see Austin glowing like a promise, and he asked again: "Make love to me."

"Whatever you need."

"So what do *you* need?" JT finally asked in return.

JT expected Austin to say something sappy. He should have known better. Austin said, "A computer. Something that will play video. Nothing fancy. No networking."

So they hazarded out of their little bolt-hole, skittish as fuck, and they stole an old Comega from a pawn shop, and JT set it up on a card table, flipped it on, and the screen went blue with nothing but a prompt. JT installed a basic LIN-Massus operating system. He had to show Austin how to work it.

Austin pulled a handful of data chips from his pocket.

"Where'd you get those?"

Austin stuttered a bit and wouldn't look at JT. He finally said, "I went back to the lab."

The words were ice in JT's veins. He turned to the door expecting those wizards to be standing there having followed Austin back. They weren't. He didn't know what was worse: that Austin had gone back to the place they'd just escaped, or that Austin had left him alone while he was sleeping. Left him alone. Here, alone. A panicked sort of rage built. He fought it down. *No.* He told himself. *No, no, no.* Because he really could have killed Austin just then. And he crossed to the other side of the dismal room so Austin's glamour wouldn't trip him up and make everything worse.

"You left me alone?"

"Only for a few minutes. A half hour. Forty-five. That was all."

"You should have taken me along."

"You wouldn't have gone. You wouldn't have let me go."

Well, that was true.

Austin turned back to the computer and slotted the first chip. He typed in commands, and the screen filled with video. It was a security camera recording of the job. Austin watched it all the way through.

When he was done, he watched it again. Then he slotted the next chip. And the next. And the next. And the days went by.

The images flickered on the screen and turned the basement into a monochrome disco. Austin tried to draw JT into his project, asking him his opinion of events and of the video he watched over and over. JT didn't want to think about it and couldn't understand why Austin would. "Why are you doing this?"

"I want to know what went wrong."

"What went wrong is we made a mistake. We trusted bad info, or old info, and we didn't survive it."

"No. That's not what happened. I'll prove it."

He left and came back with new data chips he'd recovered from who knew where. Like Austin had predicted, JT refused to go with him and tried to talk him out of it. It never worked.

Some kind of obsession had taken Austin. He rarely slept, not even that strange elven trance he had. He didn't eat. He didn't bathe except when JT complained. His eyes went sunken and dark with sleepless bruises. He looked like a heroin addict and his glamour made it look casually elegant, waifish, and lost. JT hated the look.

"You're killing yourself."

"I'm an elf," Austin mumbled, as if elves couldn't starve themselves. "We didn't make a mistake. The info was bad, but it was purposely bad. Here, look at this. And at this. And this." Austin loaded images, electricity-use spreadsheets, and old building rental contracts. "We didn't make a mistake. We were set up. Sold out. Firelight was there waiting for us."

Austin flipped through all of it so fast that JT didn't have time to process it. He didn't try. "Firelight bought us from the SFPD. Some cop made his retirement off us." He didn't know why he bothered to say these things. Austin hadn't listened to him in days.

Then once when JT awoke and Austin wasn't there, which was growing more common these days, he stared at the computer and decided to end it. He picked up a two-by-four from the random litter that filled the place, and swung it back to smash the whole goddess-cursed thing into bits.

Austin caught the end of the board. JT hadn't seen him return. He gave JT a hateful glare and wrenched it away from him, far stronger than JT would have ever expected for looking so ragged.

He threw the board into the corner, where it clattered against the concrete wall and floor. Then he sat at his computer and went back to work and never said a word.

Until days later he finally said, "I need Roan's body."

JT felt ill at the ghoulishness of it. "Well, you can't have it." It had been three months since Roan's death, and assuming her body had been taken by the police, they would have cremated her by now.

"I need her wetware. I need to break into the SFPD evidence room. They'll have pulled it before the cremation."

"What do you need that for?"

"Recording of the network before she died."

"I was there in the network, Austin. There was nothing to see. We were fooled by a virtual network while the real network prepared countermeasures."

"You told me she kicked you out before she died. You didn't see everything."

"I only missed one second. Two at most."

"A second's an eternity in the network."

"I'm not breaking into the SFPD. *You're* not. It's time for us to leave here. We'll go to Seattle or LA. Hell, even New York. We need to leave this place behind. It's killing us."

Austin shot him a deadly stare. His glamour made his sunken eyes burn like they were an orc's, and just for a moment he seemed to be someone (something) entirely different, and it broke JT's heart how far his friend had spiraled down. Austin growled, "Someone sold us out and now my sister and Grayson are dead. And have you ever wondered why we were able to escape that lab? What happened to trigger those alarms? Why was everyone dead except us?"

"No, Austin! I haven't wondered. I don't care. Please stop. Stop doing this to yourself."

Austin ignored him.

"We're alive. We're free. So let's be alive and free and get out of here."

Austin ignored him.

"I'm leaving. If you don't stop, I'll leave."

Austin might have paused in his typing just then, but if so, it was only for the barest moment, and it was easy for JT to decide it was only his wishful thinking. He knew he'd made a terrible mistake (even then he'd known)—he should never have threatened to leave.

He wrapped his few stolen clothes in a blanket (the same blanket from the lab) and stuffed them into an old duffel bag.

He stood by the door. "I'm leaving."

Austin ignored him.

"I ain't gonna watch you destroy yourself. I'm leaving."

He twisted the door knob slowly—metal, cold. He turned back to Austin. *If he's watching me, I'll stay.*

Austin wasn't.

The door's hinges were old, and it wouldn't close by itself, so he had to push it closed behind him until the latch clicked. He walked down the alley. He turned once again, telling himself, *If he's standing there, I won't go.*

Austin wasn't.

So JT left him.

Two days later he showed up at Buzz Howdy's door. "JT? Oh God! JT? What happened! Where have you been? Where's Roan?"

"Buzz? Can you make me someone else?" and then he broke down and cried.

CHAPTER FIVE

JT watched Austin top the cliff and trudge back to their rental. His hair whipped in the wind, and his shirt and khakis snapped. He was barefoot of course. Austin was always barefoot, and probably he never stepped on anything pointy out there in the grass and stone like JT would have done. The sky was gray and the Pacific was choppy, weather coming in. Every wizard they'd tried to contact had turned them down, so they'd had to drive all the way to Mendocino County.

The rental car's door closed behind Austin. "Let's go."

JT went to throw the car into gear, then grunted, frustrated. He hated rental cars. They assumed you didn't know how to drive. Their controls were locked down, and JT couldn't do anything but tell it where to go. He told it San Francisco.

It pulled from the shoulder onto the access road. Slowly. Everything the rental did, it did slowly.

JT asked, "So it didn't work out?"

"No."

"Shit, now what are we going to do? So, what happened this time? Don't tell me she was another friend of Victor's?"

"Couldn't agree on a price."

They turned out onto Highway 1. The car accelerated with excruciating care. It obeyed all the speed limits. "What did she want?"

"She wanted me to have sex with her patron."

"Who's her patron?"

"Some sea guy."

"So what's the problem?" Neither of them had ever been particularly squeamish about using their bodies to get what they wanted. First time JT ever gave a blowjob was to a cop about to arrest him. The story he told himself (and others) much later was hot. At the time he'd been scared as shit. Admittedly, trading sex for favors was a touchier subject for an elf than an orc. The elf-whore stereotype was as pervasive in pop culture as the dumb orc. Still, that had never numbered among Austin's hang-ups.

"Sea guy," Austin said again.

"So you'll get wet."

"Tentacles."

"Stop!" JT said, not to Austin, but to the car. It began to slow, too carefully, too gradually, so he shouted. "I said stop, stop!" The car got the gist and screeched to a halt. JT turned to Austin. "Tentacles? Really?"

"Yes, really."

"And you said no?"

"Of course I did."

JT told the rental to turn around.

"I should have known," Austin said.

"Real tentacle sex, Austin! Real tentacle sex!"

JT had an extensive porn collection and among its prizes was a small selection of almost-convincing tentacle-sex simulations. Sims like those were notoriously difficult to create. There were tentacle monsters in the world, of course, but none known to fuck people before eating them. So sims of sex with them were almost entirely fictional: cobbled-together collections of real sensations (the strange pulsing of a snake moving over your arm, enemas, and suffocation) hidden within the virtual reality of the sim. But here on a cold California beach, Austin had found the holy grail: real live tentacle sex, presumably without the eating.

Austin must have seen the rapturous look on him. "You are not having sex with a tentacle monster."

"One: you don't get to say who I have sex with. Two: Why not?"

"Because it's disgusting. And it sounds really unsafe."

Well of course it was unsafe. That thrill was half the point. "So you'll watch and make sure nothing weird happens."

Austin's mouth dropped open. "'Make sure nothing *weird* happens'?"

"Yeah."

"So what would you consider *weird*, exactly? Obviously not some hadopelagic thing trying to shove all twelve of its penises into your body at once—" he mimed it with his fists "—but something else . . . something weirder than that?"

"You just heard that word somewhere. You don't even know what it means."

"I know what 'penis' means. And 'twelve.'"

"I meant 'hadopelagic.'"

"I read books."

"You do not."

"I sleep with people who read books, and they teach me new words sometimes."

"Like 'hadopelagic'?"

He waved his hands dismissively. "Sleep with enough people, eventually you learn uncommon words."

Only Austin would consider sex a vocabulary-building exercise.

JT huffed, worked up. This was the opportunity of a lifetime and he wouldn't let it slide. "You can come and watch, or you can wait here if you want to. But we need magical help. So I'm getting deep-sea tentacle fucked and we're getting us a wizard."

Scorpio Dakkar was brown-skinned and had lush hair, black threaded with gray, pulled back in a bushy tail. She dressed like a beach bum: flowered shirt, cargo shorts, and sandals, which wasn't quite appropriate for this cold-water coast. Ancestry-wise she was maybe Middle Eastern, maybe Indian. JT knew better than to guess. The name told JT nothing. Wizards often took new names. Scorpio was one of the water signs in the Western zodiac. Dakkar was the last name of Jules Verne's Captain Nemo, according to some sources. She was square-shouldered, rugged like the stereotype of fishing village matrons. JT didn't often think of rugged wizards. He blinked at the sight of one.

Dakkar frowned at him.

"I'm . . . Austin said . . . Uh . . . Maybe I should go."

"You belong to Austin Shea."

"Did he tell you that? I don't *belong* to him. We're just friends. We're barely friends. Look, we need the help of a wizard and Austin said you wanted—"

"You're willing to be the sacrifice?"

"That's . . . not . . . the word Austin used."

The wizard looked him up and down. "You seem resilient."

"I'm not that resilient."

"Follow me."

When it came down to it, JT had always been a curious person, much like a cat, but with one-ninth as many lives.

JT carried his work boots stuffed with his socks. There was no real beach here, just ocean and cliff. The air was salt-filled and fresh with incoming rain. The surf rush and crash was a stadium-crowd roar. It pushed and pulled at his feet as he followed Scorpio down the narrow path along the base of the cliff to her cave.

She said, "Do you know the difference between a druid and a wizard? It's how we gain our wisdom. A druid goes on a physical journey and returns with something magical. Austin Shea wandered Winchester Mountain hungry and near death and returned with Nebraska."

JT didn't know what that meant. "The state?"

"A wizard goes on a magical journey and returns with something physical. Victor the Transmuter awoke from his astral trance blind, Horus's Eyes in his hands. He dug his useless eyes out of his head and replaced them. It was as horrible for him as you might imagine. We all make sacrifices."

Goddamn it, she knew about Victor too. "You're not close friends with Victor, are you?"

"Wizards are a small community. We all know each other. No, we're not friends. When the Awakening happened . . . a few years after because no one recognized it for what it was when it happened . . . I jumped off the Golden Gate Bridge. It wasn't a spiritual journey. I was trying to kill myself. I won't tell you why. It's none of your business, and you wouldn't understand anyway. I almost drowned, which was what I wanted, or what I thought I wanted. You have all kinds of strange dreams when you're dying. Have you read *Moby Dick*?"

"I jacked the vid."

"Which one?"

"There's more than one?"

She sighed. "It doesn't matter. The book is better. Even chapter thirty-two. For a moment I was Pip, 'and the miser-merman, Wisdom, revealed his hoarded heaps.' The Phoenician found me and saved my life, and I've served him since."

Wizards were always fucking crazy. JT should have known better. But he had to ask because no one had ever explained it to him before: "So what did you return with?"

They'd reached a narrow wet sandy beach. JT left footprints. The sand between his toes was cold.

She fished in her pocket and drew out an ancient coin.

It seemed a bit pedestrian.

"You expected something like a Tahitian pearl or a conch shell? The Phoenician isn't a spirit of water, JT. He is the first of drowned men. The miser-merman who gave to me from his hoard."

The rocky cliff to their right broke into complex grottos and outcroppings. One of the grottos was a cave, one of thousands along the Pacific Coast. It was shallow-ceilinged but deep-hewn into the cliff, swept out from the stone by uncountable tides. They entered. The floor was splotched with tidal pools, each containing their own brilliant microcosms. Between the pools stretched sandy paths. It was cool here and damp, and JT's flannel felt heavy and the sand squished under him, and everything smelled of salt and vaguely cummy like rotting snails.

Behind them something obscured the pale light from the entrance and JT turned.

There was a man there. His skin was coral. His eyes were pinpoint and pearl, hair mossy with weeds, his mouth spilled water. He didn't feel anything like death.

JT glanced over his shoulder to Scorpio Dakkar.

"Will you submit to him?" Dakkar said.

He was beautiful, carved from the sea, fish-tailed, monstrous, and beautiful. JT's "Fuck yes," was barely a sound.

The Phoenician came closer. His skin was polished, not scaled the way JT had thought. He was nude and perfect, and between his legs hung a tangle of long cocks. He took JT by the hand, and it was cool but not cold, and he leaned forward—eyes like distant stars, lanterns shining through black water—and he touched blue lips to JT's autumnal lips. He nudged a cool tongue into JT's mouth, and JT took it and closed his eyes (and still he thought he could see those pinpoint stars) and let himself be drawn toward the little god.

The tongue probed deeper than a tongue should do. It pressed against the roof of JT's mouth and down and swelled thicker, and— eyes closed—he felt the Phoenician take him in his arms, and while the god's skin was cool, there was a heat deep inside him, a soothing kind of warmth like what came from a good curry, slowly invading, slowly overwhelming. His tongue filled JT's mouth, insistent against the back of his throat. He hesitated, but JT opened wide and cocked his head back. *Oh goddess, thank you.*

Then came the strange feeling—not like being throat-fucked, but something far gentler—of that tongue slipping down into him, swelling further. He could feel it in his chest. It pulsed within him as if it was his own heartbeat. The slick goop of it gathered at his lips and slid to his chin. It tasted like the sweetest precome he'd ever tasted.

The tongue withdrew. The Phoenician stepped away. JT caught his breath, afraid that was all there was. He belched. It tasted funky.

"Take off your clothes, JT," Scorpio said.

At the cave mouth he saw Austin. He stripped. He didn't strip for the monster. He stripped for Austin. He wanted Austin to watch him get fucked by this thing. He wanted Austin to like it as much as he would.

Scorpio took his clothes and said, "You will not be able to protest once he begins."

JT shook his head; he didn't care.

The Phoenician held him again, and this time JT didn't close his eyes, but remained transfixed on those pinpoints of light.

The tangle of cocks writhed against him. They didn't feel like cocks. They felt solid, but not hard. They squirmed against his.

Something wrapped around his nuts, softer than Austin's fingers. It kept wrapping, loop after loop, circling him and pulling, balls tight and stretched. The Phoenician's arms held him. Something slick slid up the crack of his ass. A tongue invaded him again, feeling just like a tongue and nothing stranger. Until it plunged deeper.

The tugging on his nuts went painful, cremaster muscles stretched. It didn't let up but didn't get worse. He liked the feeling. He liked the feeling of whatever was sliding between his foreskin and head. He liked the feeling of it slipping into his slit. It went deeper, stretching his urethra, and that burned a little. Whatever sounded him, it wasn't smooth. He could feel the bulges and hollows of it. It slipped out and slid in and fucked his urethra. Something else wrapped his cock, coiling. It felt like a well-lubed hand. And then the tendril sounding him slid even deeper. It pushed past his prostate. The one probing his ass drove in and did the same. Everything went sore. Everything went fire and sparks.

He thought he would come right then. His whole body shook. His legs gave, and he'd have fallen except the Phoenician held him now. Held every part of him. And he kept shaking and maybe he was coming; he didn't know. He'd never been fucked like this before, so how could he know?

Slick cool ropes lashed around his ankles. The fingers that had held his had long ago dissolved into ropes that bound his hands and wrists. They drew him down, jerking him this way and that. He tried to work with them, but there was no anticipating which way they would pull, and so finally he gave in and just hung there.

All the while before him drifted the beautiful pearls of the Phoenician's eyes, and he heard Scorpio say, "'The sea had jeeringly kept his finite body up, but drowned the infinite of his soul.'"

He wondered if he'd go mad like poor Pip had done. Could you really be fucked crazy the way all the manga said?

"Austin?" he tried to say because suddenly he was scared. But he couldn't say anything. The Phoenician's tongue had invaded him. JT felt it lick the walls of his stomach. He felt it pulse as it came. (And the fact he could still breathe never struck him as amazing.)

—*Austin?* He tried to send to him, but of course Austin couldn't hear a sending. —*Austin, I think it's going to kill me.*

Then a second tentacle invaded his ass and suckers slid over his prostate one bump at a time. It stretched his colon wide, and rearranged his guts to be fucked.

He thrashed and came. The tendril deep in his dick sucked it away. The one on his balls wrenched harder, and those in his ass roiled and crawled deeper inside him. It was only beginning.

Austin watched from the cave mouth. There was barely anything of JT he could see. JT was wrapped in thick, suckered arms, some rising from the pool of water JT was standing in, some from the monster holding him. They twisted and coiled and slithered around him, here and there a flash of green skin through the loops of purple-gray; the flare of orcish eyes suddenly lost as something slid over them.

He hardly noticed Scorpio near him. She tipped her head back, smiled, and said, "His soul sings."

Austin couldn't stand it anymore. He lunged toward JT as if he'd fight the wizard's little god. She put a hand on his shoulder and said, "I don't mean the Phoenician. I mean your friend. He's quite happy right now. If you can't trust me with this, how can you entrust your lives to me at Alcatraz?"

So he stood there and did nothing as a creepy-ass godling fucked his best friend crazy.

JT's mind blurred the way orc minds blurred. He raged and fought harder. The tentacles that held him fought back. They tightened and pulled and shoved deeper and thickened. Another invaded his ass and now the three of them knotted and twisted and burrowed deeper inside him, turning the corners of his intestines, stretching them, burrowing to meet the one invading through his throat. And then a fourth joined with a sharp tearing burn of too much, and if he could have seen, if his eyes hadn't been filled with visions of the deep and drowned men floating past, hair like seaweed, he'd have seen his abdomen bulge and ripple with the things inside him. He heard the gurgle as it pumped its watery seed into him.

He came again and again, and the indescribable rapture of it was all interwoven with an ache he knew would never go away.

He fought to free himself, never succeeding, hoping to fail.

His cock felt immense, larger than skyscrapers, nuts big as planets, engorged with all the blood and come that ever was, and every part of him was stretched and torn and sucked away from him. This was the fantasy: completely and totally fucked, powerless and fucked, his whole body fucked, JT nothing anymore but a collection of holes, spread and forced open, filled and fucked by something that needed to be inside him, inside him in every goddamn way it could be inside him. Needing to be needed until there was no more JT and no more monster—neither him nor the creature—no cocks or holes, but one thing merged together in ecstasy.

And the strange beautiful errant thought rose like a singular bubble through the hadopelagic darkness of his fucking: sometimes deep in Austin's glamour, JT felt this way too.

Austin helped JT out of the cave into the cold water of the cove. When JT was done vacating whatever disgusting shit that thing had pumped him full of, Austin helped him get dressed and half carried him back to the car.

When it came right down to it, most sex was disgusting. Sure, it was hot at the time, but when it was all over, there were fluids everywhere, and often as not some of those fluids weren't the ones people liked to talk about. The both of you needed a shower, and the sheets were fucked up, and everything smelled like bleach and butt funk, and everything needed a long hot cycle in the wash.

Austin had built up quite a tolerance for gross. He liked the smell of armpit and the sour of congealed jizz the morning after. He could suck the come from someone's ass. But nothing had prepared him for this. He'd told JT it was disgusting. He'd told him. He'd *told him*, and JT hadn't listened.

JT sat in the car turned to the window, eyes closed. Every once in a while those closed eyes would scrunch and his lips would twist around his tusks.

"Are you okay?"

He mumbled, "Cramp."

Jesus fuck.

Marin County drifted by. It looked just as gray and beautifully bleak as it ever did. JT looked more and more distressed.

"Oh!" JT said, sent the autopilot the command to stop and stop fast, popped his door, and fell out onto the shoulder. And before Austin could say or do anything, he retched up something awful.

Austin kept his eyes straight forward down the road. Over and over, the horrible sounds: choke, gag, splatter. A car came up the road and swept by. JT took a loud haggard breath, said "Oh goddess, please," and started again. Between breaths he begged his goddess for mercy and promised never to do it again.

Minutes later, hours later, forever fucking later, JT calmed. He stayed down on all fours, head blissfully hidden behind the doorframe where Austin couldn't see. His back rose and fell as he caught his breath. "Towel please?"

Eyes still straight ahead so he wouldn't be tempted to look at what his friend had just puked up, he pressed the button on the glove compartment. There was nothing inside.

He unbuttoned his shirt, shrugged out of it, and handed it to JT. His skin goosefleshed, and his nipples shrunk tiny from the cool ocean breeze blowing in.

JT wiped himself clean. He climbed back into the car. He looked down at the crumpled shirt in his hands and blearily noticed, "This is your shirt."

"Angeline Donadieu. Last spring's collection."

"You love Angeline Donadieu."

Austin shrugged.

"It matches your eyes." JT sounded drunk.

Austin worked his jaw, knowing the shirt matched his eyes. That had been the point of the shirt to begin with, matching his fucking eyes.

JT handed the shirt back.

Austin took it. JT had wadded it into a ball and whatever it was he'd wiped away—monster come or whatever—was safely hidden inside. Austin rolled down his window and tossed the shirt out onto the road. He told the car to take them back home.

A few K later, Austin glanced over, and JT still looked miserable, like he was coming off an all-night binge. What if there was some kind of damage? What if one of those tentacles had ruptured something? What a fucking idiot thing to do.

"I'll be fine, Austin."

"I know." (He didn't know.)

"You're mad at me."

"It was a nice shirt."

"You're not mad about the shirt."

Austin rolled his eyes—the best lie he could make just then—and turned away. The summer-burnt heath slid past.

JT closed his eyes and let his head fall against the window. The glass cocked up his ball cap and one tusk clicked against it. He smiled sleepily, insensibly, and just before he passed out, he said, "I like it when you worry about me. I'd do it again. Just so you'd worry."

CHAPTER SIX

"**T**his is a very nice house," Scorpio told JT as she came into the old Victorian. She took a seat at the table. Everyone stared. Somehow her beach-bum clothes and knitter's bag made her the most outlandish person in the room. Either that, or it was the watery footprints she left across the living room's once pristine carpet.

At the last moment, JT remembered the unicorn horn in the fruit bowl, and he panicked a little, not wanting Scorpio to see. Evidence of a murdered unicorn—no matter how or why it might have been done—would set any wizard with any scrap of ethics on edge.

But the horn wasn't there. Austin had probably already thought of it and hidden it away.

Relieved, JT stood at the head of the table with Buzz. He made introductions, then said, "We're breaking into the castle of one of the most powerful wizards on the West Coast. If you want out now, there's the door. No backing out later." It was a formality. He didn't expect anyone to leave, and no one did.

He turned on the 3-D projector and called up a wire-frame representation of Alcatraz Island. He highlighted a solitary room well below the old Spanish Dungeons. "This room is the prison of an AI calling herself Roan. We believe she was built by Austin's sister who died two years ago. She also happens to be the only known artificial intelligence in the world to possess a glamour. We're going to free her."

He zoomed in on the room, details resolving. "The room is TEMPEST-hardened. There's no network, it's EM-shielded, magically warded, and sealed behind a Reinhardt-Baker Class II vault door."

He pulled the camera back so now they saw the TEMPEST room, then a long hall, then an adjoining room, cylindrical and stretching so far up and down that the ceiling and floor lay outside the holo-projection. The hall continued on the opposite side of that circular room, but no bridge spanned between the entrance and exit. "This room here is a bottomless pit," he said. They thought he was joking, but he wasn't.

A twenty-meter corridor connected the bottomless pit and the TEMPEST room. "This corridor is a mantrap. If we trigger the alarms on the vault door, a second door drops here at the far end of the hall, trapping us inside. We're not certain, but probably the trap will fill with neurotoxin, so we'll have to be careful."

He walked through the rest of the map. From the other side of the bottomless pit, a stairwell led up to the surprisingly unguarded Spanish Dungeons. The Spanish Dungeons led into Cellblock A. JT shifted the map around to show a floorplan of the prison/castle in its entirety.

"The exterior doors are magically warded and guarded by armor-bound spirits and traditional armed and armored guards. There are cameras at these locations." Spots flared everywhere. "We suspect that the place is haunted and Alcatraz's ghosts have been enslaved." The map pulled back even farther so the island was a hands-breadth across and the Bay took up most of the display space. "The waters around the island are patrolled by elementals, and a family of wyverns have built a nest in the old water tower."

He locked eyes with Nico, who'd gone pale. "You still in?"

Nico nodded.

JT continued: "So here's the plan. The job will be midnight of June 20, the summer solstice. The castle's magic will be weakest then, and all of the wizards should be gathered on the parade ground renewing their spells. There'll be two teams: Scorpio will carry Austin, Comet, and myself to the island."

"What?" Comet said. "No. I'm with Buzz."

"No, you're not," Buzz said. "You're with them."

Comet blinked at him like he suddenly didn't recognize his boyfriend. He said carefully, "No. I'm with—"

"Comet," Buzz warned.

Comet stopped talking, and JT could see it in his eyes: a seismic shift in his world, as if he'd never once thought he'd be taking orders from Buzz or that one of those orders might be their separation. Comet nodded a short jerky *Yes, sir, of course, sir* kind of nod, and folded his hands in his lap. He blushed a little.

JT said, "Buzz, Dante, and Nico are in the Corvette."

"The Corvette?" Austin asked.

Was everyone going to interrupt him all night? "Yes, Austin, the Corvette. That will be our command hub. I wanted to get something bigger, but Lisa did a number on us." Lisa meaning Lisa Kuang-Li, Mountain Head of the Electric Dragon Triad. "None of my suppliers will deal with me, so either we use the Corvette or we steal a car."

"So we use the Corvette," Comet said, always keen to minimize the number of crimes they were committing.

"It's in the shop," Austin said.

"You got two weeks to get it out of the shop," JT said.

Austin didn't say anything. He looked JT in the eye for a really long time. He blinked a couple of times. His cheek muscles bulged as he clenched his teeth. These were the signs that Austin had been caught in a lie and his normally mercurial brain wasn't coming up with more lies fast enough to cover the initial one.

JT put his hands on the table and tried to stay calm. "It's not in the shop, is it?"

"No."

Calm wasn't easy, not with Austin's glamour tugging at him. "Where is it?"

"I don't know."

"You lost it?"

"In a manner of speaking."

"What manner of speaking?"

"Someone stole it. Stole it back. The guy I stole it from stole it back."

Dante burst out laughing. It wasn't goddess-damned funny.

JT wasn't gonna keep calm. He went to the foyer doorway, as far from Austin as he could get and still be in the same room. The urge to hit Austin dulled.

"He had six thugs try to kill me," Austin growled at Dante. She didn't stop laughing. Everyone else, even Scorpio, cringed and tried to make themselves small.

"Six. Wow. That must have hurt," JT said, hoping it had hurt at least a little.

"Not so much, not really. They were off-the-shelf thugs. You're taking this very well."

"No, I'm not," JT said. "Okay, crime spree it is. We steal a shitload of electronics and a car."

"No," Comet said.

"We'll print one," Buzz said. "Your printer back in Greentown is functional. You and I can take Comet's bike."

"No!" Comet and JT both said.

"Last time I let you drive my bike, you wrecked it," Comet added.

"That wasn't what happened," Buzz said. "And you didn't *let* me. You *made* me."

All JT could think of was Duke. Going back to Greentown would be like poking a fucking sleeping lion. And fuck Austin, goddess bless it, *fuck* Austin. *Fuck all of them.* He wouldn't put it past them to engineer something like this just because they wanted him to patch things up with Duke. "No," he said again.

Buzz said, "Don't let your fucking ego get in the way of the job. That's Austin's role, not yours."

JT sighed. "Right. Fine. Buzz and I will take Comet's bike back to Greentown. Buzz has to program whatever we print anyway." He plopped down in a chair, brooding.

Buzz took up the lead. "While we're gone, Austin, you steal the key to those doors. We can trust you with that, right?"

Austin shrugged an *I suppose.*

"And you and Comet are going to train together. I found a gym in Mission. They got a ring and an adjoining firing and archery range. I've scheduled a daily slot for you two."

"What for?" they both said.

Austin added, "We don't need to train together. I'm sure Comet's capable."

"Oh well, thank you for the vote of confidence," Comet said, sarcastic as fuck.

Austin shrugged like it had been nothing. "Duke wouldn't have hired you if you weren't good."

"You see, Buzz? I'm good. We're all fucking good. Because Austin says so. Austin, the one who lost our car."

Buzz sighed. "You're not training together because you need to be better. You're training together so you learn how each other fights and can support the other."

"Grayson and I never trained together," Austin said.

"You fought together for four years. You started small. You worked your way up to jobs like this. None of us are starting small, are we? Look, I don't care if you two hate each other—"

"I don't hate him," Comet and Austin said at the same time.

JT would have laughed at how often the two shared the same thought, but that would have just pissed them off more.

"I just don't see why we need him," Austin added.

Buzz put his hands on the table, leaned in toward Austin, and JT had never seen Buzz snarl until now. "Go get yourself killed, see if I care. But the rest of us are depending on you too, and I ain't gonna let you get my boyfriend killed just so you can prove how goddamn tough you are. We ain't flying this job by the seat of our pants. And if you don't like my ideas, then step on up and offer your own." He put his hand to his ear. "What's this I hear? Nothing? No farts out your ass you count as ideas? Then you're fucking training!"

He stormed out of the room, spun at the door, stabbed a finger at Comet, shouted, "And you're training too!" then finished his grand exit.

JT didn't dare move, as if moving would summon Buzz back into the room and JT might be his next target.

Austin tapped his foot and looked at the table. Dante's eyes were wide, and she barely even breathed. It was impossible to tell what Comet was looking at, eyes solid blue. Scorpio rummaged in her knitting bag and produced half-made socks.

Comet shot an evil look at Austin, said, "You're an asshole," and bolted out of the room after Buzz.

The four of them sat there and said nothing. The 3-D projector hissed more nanoparticles into the air, replenishing the ones that had died. Scorpio sneezed. From down the hall came muffled talk. It rose and fell—Comet and Buzz arguing.

JT couldn't fucking believe this. All their work and planning shot to fucking hell because of Austin and his goddamn lies and everyone's fucking egos (even his own). He snapped, "He's right. You're an asshole," and followed after Comet and Buzz.

"Why am I the asshole?" Austin shouted after him. "Why isn't Comet the asshole? Because he is, you know!" A moment later he said, "I suppose you think I'm an asshole too."

He heard Dante say, "Like you even fucking have to ask."

Standing at the turn in the hall before the stairwell, JT heard low intense talk from around the corner. If they were fighting, JT wasn't sure he wanted to interrupt, so he poked his head around before barging on in.

They weren't fighting.

Comet was holding Buzz against the wall in full spread-'em pose, Buzz's shorts down around one ankle. He had one hand clamped over Buzz's mouth and the other wrapped around the guy's waist. His teeth were bared and locked on Buzz's earlobe (there'd be marks), and he was fucking the redhead as furiously as he could.

Buzz moaned and grunted into Comet's hand. Hair already gone damp with sweat curled over Buzz's eyes.

Comet whispered through his teeth, "Hotter than shit when you take control. Hotter than shit when you talk like that. Wanted to fuck you right there on the table. You're goddamn beautiful, you know that? Goddamn sexy as fuck."

Buzz squirmed back against him. His eyes opened to slits and only white showed, they were rolled back so far. Mouth covered, all his heavy breathing made his nose flare.

"You want me to take my hand away? You want everyone to hear you?" Buzz shook his head frantically no and then let go a muffled howl when Comet grinned, cocked his hips for a better angle, a few centimeters deeper than he'd been before, and pounded Buzz harder. The muscles on Buzz's thighs went tight. His calves contracted. He rose up on his toes. His legs started to shake.

Leaving the two their privacy didn't even occur to JT. If they'd cared about privacy, they wouldn't have been fucking in the hall.

JT's mouth hung open. He'd start drooling soon. His heart beat fast. His cock had thickened up and was leaking already. He could feel the cool wet in his jeans. And he couldn't look away.

Goddess, look at them. Look at Comet go to town. Look at Buzz beg for more. Comet had been in town a couple of weeks now, and he and Buzz fucked like rabbits, disappearing every few hours, showing up again flushed, sleepy-eyed. No surprise. JT knew exactly how Comet was: aggressive and chatty, the kind of guy who left bruises and scratches and got off on seeing the marks of where he'd been. His genetically-messed-with body was built to go fast and often and big and messy. JT had liked that.

He'd had no idea Buzz liked it too. And Buzz really liked it. Buzz was fucking himself on Comet. He rocked his lily-white bubble ass up and down and sweat rolled off him and his fingers clawed at the wallpaper. Chewed-to-the-quick nails scratched Victorian-style flocking away.

Was this what they did four, five times a day? How was Buzz even walking?

This was Austin's doing, wasn't it? Humans didn't feel an elven glamour the way orcs did—JT could tell where Austin was in the house by the twinge in his balls—but it wormed its way into human minds all the same, like an unexpectedly strong piña colada, and these two here were three sheets to the wind on Austin's glamour. They probably didn't even know it.

How many times had this been him and Austin? Back in the days when it had been Bell Anderson's show, Austin would make some excuse to leave their planning sessions—had to piss or something, anything—with a sidelong glance at JT, and then JT would follow a minute later. Austin would be waiting for him around the corner, cock out and hard, and JT would drop to his knees right there. And now it wasn't him and Austin anymore, it was Buzz and Comet.

Comet started cussing. He sucked at Buzz's neck between *fucks* and *oh shits*. He held his guy tight, buried his face in Buzz's hair, and went still for a moment until the shuddering started. "Oh baby. Oh God. Oh Shaggy. I love you, babe. I love you. I love—"

JT felt a hot rush in his cheeks and ears and looked away, their love embarrassing him like their fucking hadn't.

A cold dark tristesse swept him. To fight it off, he said to himself, *I did a good thing, introducing these two to each other* (which hadn't been his doing, not really, but felt like it was). If he couldn't have something good, then he could help someone else have it. And that was enough, wasn't it? His friends were in love. That was good. That was enough.

And bonus: they fucked in the hall where he could watch.

Embarrassed or not, he looked back in time to see Comet pull out, thick cock slick and come-smeared. Comet stood there, wobbly, as if he couldn't balance without Buzz's ass to prop him up. But Buzz wasn't done. He turned and threw himself at Comet, grappling him: arms around neck, legs around waist, ankles crossed above Comet's ass, and kissed Comet so hard JT heard teeth clack. Comet stumbled back under the onslaught and thumped into the wall. "Don't stop till you're dry. Fuck me, Captain," Buzz said and kept showering him with kisses.

JT snorted. Sex talk sounded stupid when you weren't the one doing it. Buzz's was especially terrible. But that was pretty daring, what he'd said there—JT wasn't sure Comet could go dry.

Comet didn't seem to think Buzz's talk was stupid. Comet hiked him up, aimed his cock, and Buzz settled down on it. Comet tried to carry him up the stairs to their room and fuck him all at the same time. He tripped on the stairs, went down on one knee, and fought to standing. He slammed into one wall, then the other. Like a drunk who might fall but not spill a drop of beer, Comet's dick never slipped out of Buzz, and Buzz never let go and never stopped begging for more.

JT almost followed them.

He didn't. He had some kind of decorum, not much, but some kind. He listened to the thumps and crashes as the two lovers wrestled their way to the second floor. Finally a bedroom door slammed closed.

Buzz's cargo shorts lay abandoned on the parquet floor. JT always had to clean up after everyone. He knelt to pick them up. Near the shorts was a thick pearlescent puddle: gush from Buzz's loosened-up hole when Comet had pulled out. If Dante stepped in it, she'd freak. He went to wipe up the mess with Buzz's shorts.

Except he didn't. Instead he glanced up the staircase and down the hall behind him. No one was watching. It was a fascinating color: white swirled with clear.

He swiped his fingers through the puddle, got them good and sloppy, and stuck them deep in his mouth. Comet's come; Buzz's ass: fucking ambrosia.

Probably he shouldn't have done that; it was like opening a door. Austin's glamour went sharp and impossible to ignore. JT's vision went fuzzy. He felt his heartbeat through his balls. The house trembled: Comet hammering Buzz's ass next floor up, shaking the whole place to its foundations. All Austin's glamour, none of it real. Real or not, it went straight to his soul and he lost himself in it.

He found himself in the dining room doorway. He held Buzz's shorts over his hard-on so no one could see, taste of come and ass still in his mouth. Dante glanced at him, and he felt stupid and exposed, but ignored her. He couldn't take his eyes off Austin:

The way his hair fell straight for ten centimeters, then began to gently curl.

The way the veins of his hands shifted position when he moved his fingers, curling over tendons and bone.

The way the stray hairs on his chin—his so-called beard—were brown and not black like JT had always thought.

The pattern made by the cartilage of his ears, as unique for elves as a fingerprint, and a tiny scar on the upper edge that JT had given him the first time he'd lost control and bit him.

Why did Austin have to lie to him? Was it ego? Was it that he didn't trust JT? JT wasn't even mad, not really (okay, maybe a bit). He was hurt.

And now Austin looked up. He saw Buzz's shorts held in front of JT and must have known right away what they were hiding because his mouth twitched into an almost smile. That rekindled JT's anger. It wasn't fucking funny, not funny at all. And he didn't want to hear Austin's inevitable suggestion that he'd *help JT out with that*. He didn't want to hear anything.

He stormed across the dining room, into the foyer toward the front door. He'd prowl the streets awhile. He'd find someone in the Haight who'd fuck him quick and dirty in an alley or a back room somewhere. Some perfect stranger. Maybe a dozen.

Austin didn't say anything. Well, of course he wouldn't. What did the elf care where JT went anyway? What did Austin care who JT fucked when he needed fucking? Austin didn't care at all.

He let the door slam behind him.

"JT! JT, I'm sorry!" But the front door slammed and Austin was too late.

He sat there for a minute or two, avoiding the looks of the others.

He told himself it didn't bother him. It really didn't. So JT was gonna find some guy to fuck him and that guy wouldn't be Austin. He liked it when JT fucked other guys, so no problem, right?

Right. He ran to the door and flung it open. Even by starlight, he didn't see JT. He was too late. "Nebraska!" he whispered. "Nebraska, let's go!"

CHAPTER SEVEN

Nebraska swiveled his little head left and right, up and down, inspecting all the people.

After JT had left him alone in that Pacific Heights basement, Austin had spent the next years wandering San Francisco just like he did now (though without Nebraska). The people around him, once solid, had gone ghostly washed-out. He saw Roan everywhere. He saw JT everywhere. He saw Grayson everywhere, and he'd never even liked the guy.

He'd pay for his food and be surprised and confused when the cashier called after him that he'd forgotten his com-card (no built-in tech to pay). He'd stumble into streets and, unchipped, BATN wouldn't account for his location and a car would screech to a stop from sonar alerts. Screech after screech of tires skidding, backed-up behind it, vehicles suddenly braked as the whole system tried to compensate for his distracted stupidity. Sometimes it seemed like the only person who knew or cared he was there was the Bay Area Traffic Net AI. He wondered if it had a name. It seemed he should know it, as much trouble as he caused her.

He'd stand for hours outside the ruins of the Hunter's Point lab where he and JT had been taken captive, returning to the scene of the crime so to speak, and he'd hope something would come out of the darkness and try to kill him. But nothing ever did.

He fucked every guy who would let him. He fucked every drone pilot. Every engineer, car mechanic, hell, even an auto-parts salesman. None were JT, and he told himself that didn't matter.

He ran jobs when he needed cash. He didn't care what he did or to whom. Sometimes his partner would try to sell him out, and Austin would have to kill them. He'd sink their bodies into the Bay or leave them bagged on certain doorsteps so the underworld would spread the word he wasn't to be fucked with. He hadn't had many friends, but when had he ever? Even JT hated him.

He'd found Nebraska because he couldn't go on that way. His life raft was a magical fox. How pathetic was that?

Like everyone who messed with sorcery or druidism, he'd heard stories about familiars. They were demons that latched on to your soul. Or they were nature spirits who warded you. Or they were nothing more than enchanted animals, magical pets. None of those stories were true. It seemed like the wizards who got one went quiet, as if they'd discovered a secret they couldn't pronounce.

Austin knew that secret. He knew why no one spoke it: Nebraska was a piece of Austin's soul cleft away before he'd even been born, and now he'd found him and Austin was that much closer to being whole. And no one spoke it because no one wanted to admit, even to themselves, that they'd once been broken and had never known it.

The fox had the perspective he couldn't have, being too close to it all. Nebraska was a silent Jiminy Cricket, never telling him how to feel, but only reminding him to do so. Surprising, how often people needed reminding. People felt so poorly these days.

A few months after Austin had met his familiar on Winchester Mountain and returned to San Francisco, Buzz had contacted him. Buzz had taken a contract with the Electric Dragon Triad to reverse engineer a "ghost," a fragment of an AI's psyche the triad's network people had somehow captured. Buzz had realized immediately the ghost was made of a handful of memories taken from Austin's sister, Roan. They'd decided to rescue it and Austin started thinking about the crew he would need to pull the job off.

Nebraska had appeared out of nowhere (the way the fox often did) and led him across town to a swank hotel where he'd leapt up on a car and posed like a hood ornament.

"What the fuck are you doing?" Austin asked him.

Nebraska never spoke, always left it for Austin to figure out what the familiar's vague actions meant. Austin hadn't been in the mood. "Come on, let's go." And when Nebraska wouldn't come, "I said let's go. Get off that fucking Corvette before some wizard sees you." Though invisible to everyone else, wizards and druids could sometimes see one another's familiars.

Then Austin noticed the car. Saw its color: a strange textureless shade of black, less a car than a car-shaped void. Saw its model and trim:

"Dawnstrike. Limited edition. Sexy as fuck. Six hundred on the magway. Full sensory integration on the exterior." That's what JT had said. And here it was.

He'd started to cry. It was the annoying kind of crying where it was mostly just the threat of crying, eyes stinging, watering just enough to be irritating, enough to make him hope no one saw because then he'd have to lie and say it was allergies. Except it was getting worse and soon he'd be unable to lie. He found a dark alley where no one would see, and he slid down the wall and hid in the darkness until Nebraska came over, and Austin held him tight and played with his fur for comfort.

"I miss him," he said aloud to Nebraska, the first time he'd ever put the feeling to words. It had somehow been easier to admit he missed his sister than to admit he missed JT. Maybe because his sister's absence hadn't been his fault. "I want him back."

Nebraska didn't say anything, as he never did. He rolled on his back and kicked his little legs up in the air begging for belly scratches like he was nothing more than a common dog. Austin scratched him.

"You don't think it's too late?"

But of course it wasn't. Nebraska wouldn't have brought him to that car if it had been too late. Would it be enough, showing up with that car and a song and dance about "one final job"? No, it wouldn't be enough. He'd have to grovel and beg. He'd have to fight to win JT back.

Well, that was okay, wasn't it? Because Austin was a fighter, a damn fine fighter.

He'd cleaned himself up as best as he could and he went into the hotel. He'd bribed a valet. "Who owns that car?"

So now Austin followed Nebraska as the fox led him to JT. He'd expected to be led to some seedy bar or sex club. Instead the fox led him to Andy's.

Austin took a seat without asking if JT cared. The table was a hightop in the bar and grill's front window. Painted letters there said *ANDY'S*, except in reverse. There were four empty pint glasses on the table.

"I thought you were going out for a blowjob."

"I was. I saw Andy's and it sounded better."

When JT chose food over sex it meant he was either depressed or high. "Look, I'm sorry I lied about the car."

"Why do you do that to me? You always lie to me. All the time. You never lie to anyone else."

"I make a living by lying to people."

"I mean your friends. You never lied to Roan or Grayson or Buzz. You don't even lie to Dante. You tell her things you've never told me."

There were all kinds of reasons he lied to people. To get what he wanted. Spite. Habit. But why did he lie to JT?

A cook called out "Jason," and that name made Austin cringe. He wanted JT to forget about Greentown and those people. He wished Comet and Dante weren't here to remind JT of all the trouble Austin had caused him. He wished he could stop causing so much fucking trouble.

JT picked up his burgers and fries at the window. He bought Austin a beer while he was up there, which was a good sign. It meant he didn't want Austin to go. He sat down and went through his hamburger ritual: tossing the bun to the side and drowning the fries he wouldn't eat in ketchup.

Austin said, "I'm a fuckup, JT, and I'm afraid you'll find out."

JT scowled at him. He cocked his head to one side and ran a pink tongue over one tusk. It made him look a bit more feral than usual.

"So sometimes I lie, hoping you won't notice."

JT's mouth twisted, and then he sighed and shook his head. "That's the stupidest goddess-blessed thing I've ever heard. I know you're a fuckup, Austin. We're all fuckups. It's not like I'm going to hate you for losing my car or doing something stupid."

And before he could stop himself, fueled by bitterness, thinking of the two years he'd spent alone, he said, "Oh really? You wouldn't hate me for doing something stupid? You wouldn't walk out on me?"

JT looked down. He took a few bites from his burger patty and washed it down with a whole pint of beer. Their silence went on a long time and the background noise took over: a chair slid over the floor, a glass *clunk* on the bar top, a sports announcer droned. JT took a deep breath. "I'm sorry I left you."

Austin had wanted to hear those words for so long, he'd dreamt them. He didn't dare move, didn't dare fucking breathe because that would break the spell of this moment. His very soul went still.

"I shouldn't have left," JT said again when Austin didn't reply. "You were right, and there was some kind of conspiracy. The job that went bad, it wasn't our fault. It was a setup. And . . . well . . . what I want to say is . . . you were right all along."

Everything began moving again, breaking away in slow motion like an avalanche.

Because that *wasn't* what he'd wanted to hear, after all. He didn't want to be right about the setup and trap. That wasn't the point.

JT called for another beer. "Go ahead. You know you want to say it."

Austin didn't say anything, too disappointed and struggling to find a way to say it.

"Austin, don't be a dick. Just say 'I told you so,' so we can get over this."

"So . . . you're sorry you left because I was right after all."

"Yes."

"What if I'd been wrong?"

JT shrugged and looked away. "You weren't wrong."

"But what if I had been?"

"I don't understand," JT said, but refused to meet Austin's eyes so he goddamn perfectly well understood.

"You said you shouldn't have left. You said you were sorry. Except the only reason you're saying that is because I was right. What if I'd been wrong? Would you still be sorry you left me?"

"I ain't apologizing for hitting you, if that's what you're getting at. You deserved that."

"Hitting me?" Austin flailed his arms in frustration. "When? You've never hit me."

"Just two weeks ago. In the woods at the fuel exchange?"

He stopped flailing. "Oh. Yeah, I forgot that."

And now there was eye contact. "You can't forget that. I laid you out flat."

"Lots of people hit me, JT; I don't keep track. I don't care that you hit me; I care about the question: What if I'd been wrong, would you still be sorry?"

A server left a new pint. JT used it to avoid him. He took a drink and then another and another, but Austin wasn't about to let him squirm away. Austin kept his gaze on him, unflinching, and JT kept his own eyes on the table, unable to look back until he finally whispered, "Yes."

He took another drink like it had been a dry mouth that had made him whisper. "I shouldn't have left. And it doesn't matter if you were wrong or right, I shouldn't have left. I was hurting, and you were hurting, and we were hurting different ways and neither of us knew what to do with the other . . ." His voice broke a bit, and he took another drink. "And instead of trying to figure it out, I left, and so neither of us had the chance to figure out anything."

"I've figured out a lot of stuff since you've been gone. Like: I pushed you away."

"Yeah, you did. You did everything you could possibly think of to push me away. But I shouldn't have let you."

They both sat there and didn't speak for a bit. Austin played with JT's food.

JT said, "It's like all those years we'd been friends, it was easy to be friends. And when it became hard to be friends, I didn't even try. I gave up." Another drink. "I'm sorry, Austin. You needed a better friend than I was." He emptied the dregs of his beer.

"I'm sorry too."

Those weren't words Austin often said. He thought he should do something to make sure JT knew he wasn't just saying them, that for once in his life he wasn't lying. He didn't know what to do. Touch his arm? Lay his fingers gently on the countertop? Cross his heart and hope to die? He tried to think of the last vid he'd seen for some clue—how the actors did it—and came up with nothing.

So Nebraska leapt onto the table.

"*Fucking goddess!*" JT fell off his stool and landed flat on his back on the floor. The stool went flying and everything around them toppled like dominoes.

The whole bar turned to look. JT thrashed around and cursed and groaned. Austin tried to right stools and tables. "Are you okay?"

"What the fuck is that?"

"You can see him?"

"Of course I can fucking see it!"

"It's a him, not an it." Austin helped JT up. He tried to wave the attention of the crowd away, knowing to them this was nothing but a drunken orc falling off his barstool. They couldn't see Nebraska at all. He called for more beer. The bartender looked doubtful.

JT settled back onto his stool. He stayed a full meter from the table. Nebraska sat in the center of it, golden and shining and perfectly adorable in the way that he was. He licked a paw and ignored them both, star-shine eyes bored as ever.

"What is that?"

"That's Nebraska."

"Nebraska? Like Scorpio said. Is that your familiar?"

"Yes. It's my familiar."

"You got a familiar."

"A few months ago."

"You always made fun of—"

"I was *alone.*"

JT shut the fuck up, thank God. Austin saw in JT's eyes all the working of his mind through the chain of events, all the cause and effects that had led Austin to Nebraska, and his own role in it. He said, "I'm lucky I met Duke and Comet and Dante when I did. I'd have gone crazy otherwise." And Austin knew JT understood. That was why they should be together: because JT understood.

JT said, "Does he eat popcorn?"

"No, he doesn't eat popcorn. He doesn't eat anything. He's a familiar."

JT stood and went to the bar where they had a popcorn machine and scooped some into a bag and came back.

"I said he doesn't eat popcorn."

"Does he bite?" JT put a few blown kernels into his hand and held them out tentatively.

"Yes! He bites. And he doesn't like orcs."

Nebraska had never bitten anyone but a wizard named Victor, and of course the traitorous little bastard didn't bite JT at all. He sniffed at JT's hand and then at the popcorn. He tongued up the kernels. Austin was fairly sure Nebraska couldn't eat anything and was just faking it to spite him.

JT grinned a scary tusk-filled grin, the happiest Austin had seen him in forever. But an orc fawning over a cute animal, well that was just disgusting, that's what that was. "Goddess, he's adorable. How did *you* end up with him?"

Austin caught the sarcasm fine. He ground his teeth and worked his jaw. He took a very long drink.

Grandfather had told him: *"Most will not see him. The ones who care for you, though, he might choose to reveal himself to them."* Austin should have known that had been a fucking warning.

CHAPTER EIGHT

Pier 39 was part of the Amazon enclave, but the corporation's contract with the city designated the pier as a tourist destination so noncitizens were allowed to enter on a day pass. Under a fake ID created by Buzz, Comet guzzled wine at the bar of a swank restaurant called Pierless 39. The name was a pun, ha ha.

His body processed alcohol faster than he would normally drink it. To stand any chance of getting drunk, he had to put some serious effort into it.

So after one bottle, he still wasn't feeling it. He didn't bother with the glass anymore. The bartender should have cut him off but mostly seemed amused.

Austin's thoughts appeared in his head. —*Look around. I can't see anything but that bottle and that hot bartender you're staring at.* Austin was linked into Comet, monitoring him from outside the restaurant via a cracked-screen tablet like Comet was some green recruit.

Comet hadn't been staring. He'd been thinking about Buzz and Duke and home and wishing he was there.

He looked around like Austin had asked. Pierless was made of glass boxes overlapping and superimposed. It hung out over the water, like a tower of ice cubes falling into the sea. Discreet signs on the restaurant door warned customers of possible vertigo. Out in the Bay, Alcatraz Island glittered with its evil fairyland castle. Farther in the distance, Godzilla splashed through the shallow water.

Within hours of City Netspace going public access in the late fifties (what people now called the Fog City Renaissance), Godzilla had appeared. The network hack had rampaged through the Netspace's virtual re-creation of San Francisco, and once he had thoroughly virtually trampled the town in a pattern of destruction that precisely mirrored the quake of 2025, the great lizard had wandered into the Bay and there he'd remained in all the years since.

—*You're accessing Netspace?* Austin asked. Since Austin could see everything Comet could, he'd also have seen Godzilla.

—*Sure. It's fun.*

—*I've never imagined the words "Comet" and "fun" in the same sentence.*

—*Why do I have to do this? I'm only here for the fighting, okay?*

—*And Buzz's ass.*

Comet ignored him. —*I ain't a thief.*

—*You have to do this because I'm pretty and people remember me. You're just you.*

Comet had glowing blue eyes and heat-sensitive hair. He wasn't "just" anything. —*Firelight knows who I am.*

—*Firelight isn't going to tell his minions to be on the lookout for the unarmed man who kicked the shit out of him while he was a dragon. Firelight ain't gonna breathe a word of that to anyone. There's your mark.*

The Thousand Suns didn't have a thousand members. They had about a hundred, which was still a lot of wizards. New members were accepted regularly. It was a huge honor, like getting into an Ivy League school, and it was a tradition to celebrate with family and friends at some public venue while wearing the symbol of their achievement and privilege: their robes. It was one of the very few times a wizard would wear them in public.

And there seated amid a collection of well-wishers was a young wizard who'd just been awarded membership to the Thousand Suns. Comet's mark.

Comet took his bottle of wine and left the bar.

A message came in from Duke. Messages came in from Duke all the time. He'd ignored all of them because JT had asked him to. But this time he missed home, and maybe he wasn't as immune to the wine as he'd thought, and fuck JT for putting him in this position in the first place.

—*Duke*, he answered.

A long silence before Duke responded.

—*I assume this means you're not in jail.*

—Not yet.

—You're not going to tell me what you're doing?

—No. JT asked me—

—You mean Jason.

—His real name's JT.

—I know his real name. I know everything about him. I could help.

—He doesn't want your help. He thinks the price tag is too high.

—What fucking price tag? There ain't no fucking price tag.

—Isn't there?

Comet wove crookedly across the glass floor of Pierless 39. The bar floor was tiered and packed with high and low tables so everyone had a vertiginous view. Newbies and drunk people often spoke as they sent, so he did it too. "You help him out and he owes you a favor, isn't that the way it works?" He was loud enough that people looked his way as he threaded through tables toward a balcony. He was angry. He might be drunk. It was easy to be loud.

—He's a friend, there's no fucking price tag.

"You know he can pilot six drones simultaneously? You know he took down a master-piloted Atari Koroshiya 036 with a pack of utility drones?"

—Yes, I know that.

It was easy to be stupid. "Don't tell me you haven't thought of getting him on the Squad. Don't tell me you haven't been scheming a way to get him under your thumb."

It was a beautiful day, midafternoon skies blue as blue got, so the balcony was packed and you'd bump people if you weren't careful. Comet bumped a lot of people.

Duke didn't respond.

"Oh my God, you really have been thinking of it. And here I thought JT was just being paranoid. Duke, you fucker. You manipulative fucker! You know JT wants to come home. He wants to go back to Greentown so badly you can see it in his eyes. Except he isn't gonna come home, and do you know why? Because of you!"

Comet jostled tables and people alike. Glasses rattled and sloshed and everyone scowled at him. He apologized loudly.

He wove to the pushed-together tables where the wizard's party was celebrating, a good twenty people, all of them dressed in Armani and Ousier Brie, except for the guest of honor in his ceremonial wizard robes.

Duke sent nothing. He was so quiet that Comet had to check to make sure the connection still held.

Comet had work to do. He couldn't afford this distraction now. He was supposed to be pretending to be an angry drunk, not actually becoming one. "I should never have answered your message," Comet said, breaking the connection and waving his arms around in not-quite-pretend frustration. He swung his arm out just a bit too far, just the way he'd planned, and knocked the wizard upside the head with the bottle, far harder than he'd planned. Wine splashed everywhere. The wizard stood and shouted curses (mundane ones, thank God). Wine ran in streams down his nose and his formal robes.

The rest of his table, elegantly dressed men and women in suits, rose slowly and scowled at Comet.

The robe he'd just ruined was fantastically expensive. A wizard's formal robes were of the finest fabrics, hand-sewn, hand-embroidered. Wizarding wasn't a cheap craft. The embroidery was gold and done in flames and coiled dragons. The thread was discolored by wine. The velvet and silk was patchy with red. "Oh God. Really, I'm very, very sorry. I'm a bit drunk. Maybe drunker than I should be. Look, I can pay for that. I really can. I'm ... uh ... Shen Nu with CrossPac Exports and we can pay. We're good for it. Please allow me?" And he held out his hand for a data transfer just like Austin had told him.

The wizard sneered at it because of course he didn't have the built-in tech to accept a transfer. The move had been purposefully chosen to make Comet look like more of an idiot.

So Comet begged for a pen and paper and debased himself as well as he could as he wrote down contact info for the accounting department of CrossPac Exports. It was hard to concentrate. He'd just yelled at Duke and disconnected without warning.

There were a few centimeters of wine left in the bottle. He tried to drink it, but the wizard snatched the bottle from his hand and said, "Perhaps you should go home."

Yeah. Yeah, probably he should.

Comet was moody by the time he met Austin on the pier. They wove through the tourists back into the public city.

"That was some grade-A acting back there. Sounded just like you were actually arguing with someone." Austin said it in the tone that made it perfectly clear he'd known Comet hadn't been acting. In the heat of the moment, Comet had forgotten Austin had been networked in and could hear everything he said.

They walked down the pier. They passed a class of children buying gelato like he and Austin were everyday people and not thieves.

"I feel like a criminal now."

"You spilled wine on someone. That's not a crime."

"I feel like an asshole, then."

"And that's never bothered you before. No reason to let it start now. If it helps, that guy you just doused with wine is celebrating his initiation into an organization that kidnapped JT and tortured him. So let's keep things in perspective."

Two days later a $400 charge from Davis Dry Cleaning hit the account. The bill was paid and then CrossPac Exports disappeared into the quantum digital foam from whence it had come.

Davis Dry Cleaning: Small businesses always had shit for security, thinking no one would ever hack them, so Buzz was able to do it in less than five minutes. He didn't touch anything, didn't steal a dime, just recorded the MAC address of a delivery drone.

Dante and Nico set up shop at the corner of Fillmore and Geary, which was still city property because it was an ugly neighborhood and no corporation wanted to shell out the money to support a transportation hub.

Dante had never been in a city this big. Nico had tried to tell her that SF wasn't a big town, seemed that way but wasn't, but Dante couldn't believe it.

This neighborhood here felt different than the Haight. Both felt worn to her, but the Haight felt worn like a good pair of jeans. Fillmore was like an old transmission in a car whose owner didn't care.

She was the only orc in sight and that made her nervous. And sure, there weren't a lot of orcs in the Haight either (there were tons of elves), but this was different. People would glance at her from time to time, and she'd try to act nonchalant but didn't know what nonchalant was. Did she nod and say hi? Did she look away and ignore them? Did she glower and tell them to mind their own business? She tried to follow Nico's lead, but Nico was an elf, not an orc, and he met every glance with a cocky bring-it-on grin that only he could do and would have looked feral on her. She told herself she had every right to be here, which was true. She told herself she wasn't doing anything wrong, which wasn't.

The corner of Fillmore and Geary was a transportation nexus same as it had always been. Delivery drones buzzed above her, large for airborne drones. They had to be to carry their payloads. Most of it was take-out food delivery, but some were corporate courier services and others were a couple of days' worth of groceries. Some were crime monitors and some were decoys, empty except for paint bombs because kids liked to fuck with the drones.

Kids like Dante.

Business drone traffic was relegated to mid-altitude travel—ten to twenty meters above ground. And there was enough of it that it had to be managed the same way passenger and freight vehicles were managed: by the Bay Area Traffic Net. Each drone sent its MAC address and its GPS data to the BATN drone management AI. The AI cranked its analysis and returned navigation directives. Collisions were a thing of the past.

Dante's personal drone spun quietly over her head. Unlike cars and business drone traffic, personal drones weren't required to be managed, but were required by law to fly beneath the business traffic so as not to interfere. The rotors of Dante's drone kicked up a light breeze across the street-side table she and Nico had been sitting at for an hour. The drone's payload was a dozen rolls of extra-strength Charmin.

"This is boring," Nico said.

"So was watching you case an antique store for a week. Sometimes the job is boring."

Dante had spent a lot of time with Nico over the last several days. He was quiet, which surprised her. He had quiet hobbies. He listened to music, volume way down. When the recording part of his vinyl records ended, the needle fell into a repeating groove of hissing and pops. He'd listen to that for ten minutes or more as if that white noise held just as much data as the grooves that preceded it. He modeled virtual art. He worked on JT and Austin's secret weapon and wouldn't show it to her. She wanted to ask him to draw her, but was afraid he'd take it wrong, so she didn't. She was halfway smitten and knew it. It made her extra cautious—touchy maybe—because she knew perfectly well what guys like him did to girls like her.

—*Here it comes*, she sent and flagged a drone two blocks away with a red augmented-reality tag only they could see. She ran a quick scan of the street looking for monitor drones, but it was hard at a glance to tell those from any other. She'd just have to risk it.

She sent her drone higher and let it drift out to the street as if she weren't paying attention and the wind was pulling it away, though there wasn't much wind. She flipped her vision to its camera. And when the aug-flagged drone got near, she paced it with her drone and lifted hers right up beneath it. She didn't collide the two.

She put in a request to BATN to add her drone to its management. BATN tried and spat an error: duplicate MAC address. The flagged drone kept moving. She followed it with her own drone, carefully tracking, one beneath the other so that their GPS locations were practically identical within a standard margin of error. Around her, no one noticed. Drone traffic was so common it might as well have been invisible.

She executed the program Buzz had written for her. It hammered BATN with add requests. BATN responded by blocking the MAC. The flagged drone stopped. She waited thirty seconds for the block to time out and tried to slip in a management request before the flagged drone's recovery protocols re-sent its own.

She didn't time it right. The flagged drone resumed its course.

"Oops," Nico teased.

She ignored him, matched up the drones again, and executed the program a second time. She'd only get so many chances at this before the system recognized her hacking attempts for what they were.

The flagged drone stopped.

Nico needled her, "Are you nervous? Don't be nervous."

"Shut—" she snapped and mistimed her signal again. She glared at him, hoping her tusks made her fierce. "Shut the fuck up, okay!"

He held up his hands in surrender and kept quiet.

Third time was a charm. Her signal beat the drone's, BATN accepted it, and her drone was swept away on the river of flying dinners, groceries, and toilet paper.

Everyone in San Francisco hated BATN; they hated the loss of autonomy the system cost them. The fact that it saved hundreds of lives every year and who knows how many millions in traffic-related business costs only barely balanced opinion in its favor. No matter what the logs might imply, no one would ever believe that thieves had hijacked a drone by spoofing a MAC address and causing a network rejection. They'd blame it on a glitch in BATN's AI.

The flagged drone hung there in the air, forgotten by every system.

"Now what?" Nico said. The drone was fifteen meters up and there was no way to reach it.

Dante sighed. "We wait for the batteries to die."

"Are you fucking kidding me?"

"No."

Nico slumped in his chair and popped his tongue piercing in and out of his mouth. "Worst. Crime. Ever."

Dante was practically busting with excitement as she watched Austin open the drone's payload crate. She was pissed he wouldn't let her do it. She'd been the one to steal it, after all. She expected grenades. A rocket launcher maybe. Or maybe some kind of software that turned people into goop. This was like fucking Christmas, and Dante had never had Christmas before.

Austin unfolded the tissue paper from whatever it contained. It didn't look like grenades. He lifted out a dry-cleaned wizard's robe.

"Laundry? You fucking had me fucking steal someone's fucking bathrobe? What do you want me to steal next? His skid-marked underwear?"

"This," Austin said happily, "isn't laundry. This is our key into Alcatraz." He pulled it on and it fit perfectly of course, and he threw the hood up and over his head and did a little spin and laughed melodramatically evil.

It wasn't fucking funny. "Don't you *ever* tell Nico about this. *Ever.* It was grenades. I stole a boxful of grenades."

CHAPTER NINE

It had been only a few weeks since JT had driven County Road 3140. It felt like years. The road was covered in wind-blown orange dust, and it ran over high plains spotted with tough grass and scrub that didn't need much water to live. It ran past JT's old place.

JT released tiny drones that sped ahead of the bike. They scanned the fuck out of the place before he let Buzz take them within ten K. He wasn't worried about Firelight. He was worried about Duke.

Buzz said, "We're gonna be here a week. He's gonna find out."

Satisfied there were no spies, they snuck into the place—into JT's own home—in the middle of the night.

The last time he'd seen it was through the rearview camera of the Corvette as he and Austin fled from Valentine, comatose Dante in the back seat. Coming back to it now made him heartsick.

The place was a wreck, and all that damage was just the incidental tip of the iceberg of everything he had lost—his home, his business, his friends—and he wanted it all back. And maybe it was a boring life, but barring the risks Comet took with his job, none of his friends were likely to die from boredom. And maybe Duke was an asshole sometimes, but he wanted Duke back too.

Buzz was right. Duke was going to find out they were there, but JT wasn't going to welcome it when it happened.

He stood in the center of the compound's empty lot and would have cried had Buzz not been there. So instead JT did what he always did when he was upset. He went to work.

He unleashed a horde of repair drones. Valentine's attack had been precise. The control room for the 3-D printer was trashed, but the printer itself was intact and undamaged just like Buzz had said.

The wiring in the main house was shorted out and the home's virtual intelligence dead, but the fires had been small and limited to scorching, and the building was fine if you ignored the faint but lingering sharp smell.

By morning he'd restored what electricity he and Buzz needed and had fired up the AC, Buzz unused to the heat. They slept, JT in his bedroom, Buzz on the couch. He heard Buzz mumble-talking to Comet over the net, vocalizing occasionally the way people sometimes did. JT dreamt strange dreams of dungeons and unintelligible whispers from adjoining cells that made him stir, half-woke, sweating, heart pounding.

The afternoon sun was blazing hot when they arose.

They repaired the printer control room as best as they could. The bank of monitors was broken to pieces, but the floor holo-projector worked and most of the peripherals. He cloned a new computer from a backup, loaded the printer's slurry reservoirs, and ran some tests.

In the garage, huge and empty, Buzz placed an ancient computer on a rickety card table in the exact center of the space. It looked far too much like the computer he'd set up for Austin years ago, and the sense of déjà vu was so strong it nearly made him sick. They suspended concentric aluminum rings from the ceiling and hung EM-shielding foil like they were shower curtains. Buzz made damn sure JT understood that under no circumstances was he to enter the garage with his internal wireless active. In fact, just stay the fuck out entirely.

JT knew a makeshift virus lab when he saw one; he hadn't needed to be told.

An AI's psyche required an elastic architecture, the kind of peptide/DNA architecture found in cybernetic wetware. Buzz was going to create a virus that when released into the world would infect the wetware of tech-saturated people like himself and JT, then carve away and dedicate a tiny bit of processing space for the RoanAI to use. Among the treasures in the Blue Unicorn's data payload were a set of API definitions, the rules programmers needed to make one program communicate with another. Each person infected would become a node in a vast machine—the RoanAI's mind.

JT watched Buzz boot up his computer. The old-fashioned monitor flickered green and gave a command prompt, its operating system barely anything at all. It reminded JT of another computer long ago. "Five hundred thousand people is a lot of people to infect with a virus."

"Five hundred is a bare minimum. The Death Star specs gave a safety tolerance of about eight hundred to create a stable cloud."

"Eight hundred thousand people infected by Roan," JT muttered. Sometimes it felt like Buzz didn't have the same set of ethics as normal people.

"This isn't Roan. It's an AI built from her memories."

"I know that."

"At least one of you does."

"What do you mean?"

"Austin. I don't think he understands that the RoanAI isn't Roan. He doesn't get it that she's just an AI using Roan's memories as a structure. He thinks we're saving his sister."

Where Buzz had gotten that idea, JT didn't know. Austin didn't think that. Austin was adamant the thing they were saving *wasn't* his sister. It was JT who wasn't so sure.

Buzz typed commands into the computer via keyboard, not interfacing directly.

JT hazarded, "Well . . . I mean . . . it's not an unreasonable idea, right? I mean, it could be? Isn't that possible? She uploaded herself?"

"You can't upload yourself."

"I mean normal people, no. But she was 3djinn and you guys know all kinds of things other people don't know. She could have uploaded."

"You can't upload yourself."

"You don't know everything!"

"You just said I did!" Buzz swiveled around on his chair. "You can create a simulacrum, that's all you can do. You can plaster together simulated sensation on a memory framework, and flip a switch and hope everything integrates, but there are chaotic variables that instantly degrade the entire structure. Simulations last less than three seconds as recognizable personalities and become aberrant. That whole dream of immortality is bullshit."

Goddess, JT hated it when Buzz started talking like a fucking science professor.

Buzz turned back to his work. "It took twenty-two years to make my mind, JT. Twenty-six to create yours. Twenty-nine to create

Comet's. Intelligence is a *process*, not a fucking *state*. And it's not just a process of neurons firing in a particular order. It's an interaction between you and your environment. You can't snapshot it and copy it like an image."

JT didn't want to hear any more. He wasn't used to feeling stupid and he didn't like it. "All right, I get it! All I'm saying is you can't blame Austin if he believes she's really Roan. But don't worry, because he doesn't. Why does everyone always worry about Austin? Austin is fine. The way Austin always is."

Maybe he said that with too much of an edge, because Buzz turned back again and gave him a narrow, suspicious look. "Don't tell me that *you* think she's Roan."

He didn't. Not really. But he wanted her to be. And though he'd never admit it to anyone, it wasn't just because he missed her and wanted her back. It was the entire idea of uploading one's self that he wanted to be true. Because if Roan could do it, then JT could do it too. Then he could be anything he wanted to be. Anything other than a monster. "No, of course not."

Buzz stared a few long seconds as if he could tell whether JT was lying. Then he went back to work. He typed with two fingers; keyboarding was a skill few had anymore.

JT said, "It won't hurt them, will it? I don't think Roan would have wanted something she built from her own memories to hurt eight hundred thousand people."

"This isn't gonna hurt anyone. It's the most harmless virus ever made."

"It turns almost a million people into a parallel machine to process an AI's psyche. How is that harmless?"

Buzz rolled his eyes like JT was some naive kid. "Those people are already infected. *You and I* are already infected with a half dozen viruses just like the one I'm going to make. Where do you think the Collective lives? You think all those rogue AIs got together and bought a server farm in Ohio or something? No. They're cloud-based. Parasitic. Symbiotic if you're feeling generous. Why do you think they haven't killed off humanity like any sensible alien life form would? They live in our heads. 3djinn estimated that point eight percent of my personal network traffic is AI subroutines. And if we do this right, pretty soon the RoanAI will bump that to point nine. She'll live in us. Isn't that cool?"

Buzz smiled, genuinely happy, as if he couldn't think of any better afterlife than that.

Midday, hungry, JT returned to the house. He wiped Goop from his hands with a rag and threw it on the table.

He'd printed the microwave antennas and smaller electronics they needed. The truck was printing in pieces, everything on schedule.

The place was half-dark, front window polarized, and Buzz—who worked night owl like every hacker ever did—was crashed on the couch, barefoot but clothed, grumbling and twitching like he was caught in a bad dream. So JT went over to wake him, but it wasn't a bad dream.

A grand ol' hard-on sported in Buzz's shorts.

Sim stim worked by intercepting neural signals and modifying or replacing them. When someone went deep like Buzz often did, neural signals from sensory organs (including your skin) went nowhere; vice versa, signals from brain to limbs went nowhere either. If you were in a simulation that required you to run and you sent that signal to your legs, you wanted your virtual legs to move and not the real ones. But the shunting of signals wasn't absolute. If the signal was intense enough, some of it would slip through the neural blockade and limbs would twitch, or lips might form barely sensible words. If the signal was intense enough—the way sex usually was.

This wasn't a bad dream. Good money said this was Comet cyber-fucking the shit out of Buzz.

Buzz whispered half-formed curses. His toes curled and stretched. His hips shifted and his fingers clenched and released.

JT sighed. He went to the fridge and got himself a beer.

Buzz groaned garbled words, louder than all the rest, and JT rolled his eyes and tipped the beer back. He made himself a turkey sandwich. He ate it at the table and watched Buzz, not feeling the slightest bit embarrassed.

He wished Austin were here. Austin would have teased Buzz mercilessly. He'd have found a magic marker and written obscenities on him. And then he'd have proposed a race or something equally stupid: Who would come first, JT fucked by Austin or Buzz fucked by Comet?

It was the kind of bullshit they'd done years ago to Grayson before Grayson had been filled full of holes.

Buzz made clicking noises. It was either the *C* of *Comet* or the *K* of *fuck*. He gave a shuddering sigh. Breathing was still breathing no matter how the rest of the signals were routed. JT took a bite of his pathetic sandwich. He'd used the last of the turkey and there hadn't been enough.

Look at Buzz there. Buzz was cute, sure, but socially hopeless and nerdy. Comet, on the other hand, was so damn cocksure and had every reason to be. The two of them were so terribly mismatched no one would have ever guessed them together, but they were. One thousand K between them and they still were.

What if he and Austin had that? Was it such an impossible thought after all?

Goddess, it felt like it. Sometimes. Nearly all the time. An elf and an orc together like that?

He almost sent a message to Austin's tablet, except he couldn't even pretend he needed an update on Dante or the laundry job. Comet and Buzz were linked up 24/7, it seemed, and JT already knew everything. And Austin was notoriously hard to contact anyway if he didn't have his damn tablet on him, which he often didn't. So no, he wouldn't call. What would he say?

I miss you. I'm bored when you're not around. He could say that. How would Austin respond to that? He couldn't even imagine.

Buzz gasped and sat up abruptly. He heaved heavy breaths. He muttered things and swiped his hands clumsily as if he were tangled in spiderwebs.

Buzz had come.

JT yawned.

Buzz blinked. He laughed and whispered something meant for Comet that JT couldn't hear. He sat on the edge of the couch, shakily, saw JT watching him, and said, "Shit." He covered his crotch with a throw pillow. "Oh shit. JT. Shit. I'm. Uh. Bad dream."

"Did you know ninety percent of network traffic is porn bots fucking other porn bots?"

Buzz just sat there and blinked, still probably shaking the Comet fuzz out of his head.

"Oh for goddess's sake, Buzz, it ain't like you and Comet try very hard to hide it. I've watched you guys fuck a half dozen times by now."

"What?"

"Oh please. Like you didn't know. Don't seep on my pillow."

Buzz threw the pillow onto the couch. His cargo shorts were unstained. JT had blown Buzz before, so knew what Buzz's cock looked like, and now that he paid closer attention, that bulge in Buzz's pants was a bit bigger and lumpier than it should have been. JT knew exactly what was going on: Buzz had stuck a washcloth down his shorts to keep from messing them while he was deep under.

Buzz went to the washing machine that was to one side of the kitchen, most of JT's place being the one large room. He turned away from JT, dug his hands down his shorts, and pulled out a wad of cloth. He tried to hide it as he threw it into the wash, but JT saw it just fine. It wasn't a washcloth. It was a gray sock with a red stripe on the toe. Buzz closed the washer door and stood in front of it as if to hide it.

"Was that my sock?"

"I'm gonna wash it."

"Use a washcloth!"

"Socks work better."

"Then use your own!"

"I didn't pack enough!"

"How many of my socks have you come in?"

Buzz went bright red. "Comet's modified, okay? And he and Austin have been sparring, and when Comet gets home he's in a mood, and ... well ... he's how Comet is, you know. So. A lot of socks. I've been washing them."

JT wriggled his toes in the socks he wore. He'd thought Buzz had been washing his clothes just to be nice.

"You know what? Why don't you get yourself a towel and sleep in my room where you can take off your shorts and be naked and jizz as much as you want, and I'll sleep on the couch and you leave my socks alone?"

Behind them, a sarcastically slow golf clap. Buzz's eyes went wide, and JT turned to see Duke Mason. "Well, I'm glad we got the come-sock problem resolved."

Buzz tried to escape. "You guys need to talk, I can tell, so I'll just go."

"Like fucking hell you will. I own you, Vixen." Duke used the Reindeer Squad code name Buzz hated. "Sit down."

Buzz sat down on the couch like he'd been pushed down.

JT said, "How'd you know we were here?" He gave Buzz a dirty look. "Did you tell him?"

"Vixen didn't tell me shit. I knew because I drive past here every day wondering where my boys have gone and if they're alive or dead, hoping eventually you'll come back and I don't have to have a funeral with no body. That's how I know." To Buzz: "You're talking to Comet right now, I can tell. You tell him he's in deep shit for mouthing off to me."

A moment passed where JT was pretty sure Buzz did as he'd been told.

"And you've been fighting Prancer," Duke said to Buzz.

JT hadn't known about that. Buzz shrugged sheepishly. "She's been trying to find us. She's not bad. I've had to do a lot of work to keep us hidden. We've been a little sloppy."

"We didn't want you to get involved." JT said.

"Well, I'm involved. Four of my people—"

"Three. Dante's not yours."

"Two. I don't know if you are either."

Fair enough.

Duke said, "*Two* of my people are involved. So I'm involved."

"Comet wouldn't be there if I had any choice," JT said.

"He wouldn't be there if *I* had any choice," Duke said. He crossed the room to the kitchen and dug a beer out of the fridge. He tossed it to JT, and JT popped the top with one tusk and gave it back. The top clattered on the bare concrete floor.

Duke sat at the little table in the living room. He was huge and made the chair beneath him look like it had been sized for kindergartners. He took a drink. No one said anything. JT braced himself. He had imagined the worst: the guilt trips, blackmail, bribery, every brand of emotional manipulation in the book. He'd rehearsed responses to all of them in his head for weeks now, and he was still unprepared for what to say.

Duke took another drink. The bottle was half-empty. "I just realized I've never been here before. Two years I've known you and I've never been in your house. You always came to mine. You got no taste in decoration."

JT didn't rise to the bait.

So Duke went on: "I spoke to Comet."

"Fucking goddess," JT grumbled.

"Comet gets angry with me all the time. He never says anything. He lets it build up, days, weeks, months, until he explodes." He tipped his bottle Buzz's way. "You remember that, Vixen. Don't let him build up. Well, this was one of those times, and he exploded the way he does, and he reminded me in very few words that I'm a prick."

Duke shifted in his chair and frowned. "Probably there are reasons I'm a prick. Only child, zero-gen-orc, bad-parents reasons. They don't matter. I'm an adult, and I could choose to not be a prick if I wanted, but I don't."

"So when Comet and that fucker there," he said, pointing at Buzz, "drop off the map chasing after you and your elf, and the next thing I know I'm getting a folder filled with background on you, and I looked through that folder, and Jesus God what a résumé that was, the first thing I thought was how I was going to get you working for me, directly for me, on the Squad. Because you're a cold killer and a genius, and I can use people like you. So it turns out, you were right, Jason. I'm exactly the person you imagine me to be."

And hearing Duke say that, hearing that low bass growl say that JT was a killer, was probably the most devastating thing JT had ever heard. Almost as devastating as hearing Duke confess that he was a shitty person. It was one thing for JT to think those things about Duke, another to hear Duke voice them himself.

"I don't think you're—"

"Shut up, JT."

JT. Duke had called him JT, and it felt like a chapter of his life closing off.

"And so Comet reminded me that I'm a prick, and I thought about it, and I decided just this once that's not who I wanted to be. I decided I miss your company and want you back here in Greentown where you belong."

JT floundered. "I don't know what you mean."

"Do you want to come back?" Duke said.

"Yes."

"If you come back, I'll pretend I know nothing about you, except the ID Vixen built. I won't pressure you into joining my company or working with the Reindeer. You can build your fucking cars if that's what you want. Such a fucking waste of talent, but if that's what you want. And I'll do what I can to protect you from people like Valentine, or whoever else there might be."

JT couldn't speak. His throat had tightened horribly.

"Don't get me wrong. You hurt me, JT. I wish you hadn't lied to me. I might understand why you lied, but I wish you hadn't. I wish I'd been someone you hadn't needed to lie to."

Duke emptied the bottle and went to the door. "One last offer: Do you want my help with this whatever-you-got-going-on or not?"

"No."

"All right, then." He had to turn sideways to fit through the door. He gave JT a glance, eyes lightning-bolt gray, and said. "If you get either of my boys killed—Comet or Vixen—don't come back."

"I won't let them die, Duke. No one's gonna die."

The huge orc nodded, gray braids falling over his shoulder. "Good." He patted the doorframe like the house was a pet too long without its master. "Good." And then he left.

JT buried his head in his hands.

After a few moments of quiet, Buzz said, "Are you okay?"

"No." JT had thought he'd prepared himself for everything. He hadn't prepared himself for the impossible chance that Duke would forgive him.

CHAPTER TEN

A ustin sat on the windowsill of his room on the third floor of the house and watched JT work. He liked watching JT work.

JT and Buzz had been away for ten days, and Austin had been edgy the whole time, as if JT would decide to stay in Greentown and never come back. Even after overhearing the conversation between Comet and Duke, that nagging fear was there.

But they'd come back after all.

Of course they had. It was just Austin's nerves, thinking otherwise.

JT had parked his newly printed truck street-side, driver's-side wheels cocked up on the curb to make room in the road, the wheelbase was that broad. The truck was so high off the ground, JT had installed a rail beneath the front bumper, something to stand on so he could work on the engine. He'd climbed the monster wheel and scooted around the standing rail, popped the hood, and was tinkering with something beneath it. The truck was brand-new, probably smelled like hot plastic, so what might still need work, Austin couldn't guess. Probably JT just liked the feel of his hands in the engine.

Partly Austin liked watching a skilled craftsman practice their craft. (He even liked watching Comet practice, truth be told. At least when he could do it without the fucker knowing.)

Mostly, though, he liked watching JT bent over like he was. JT filled out a pair of jeans like they'd invented jeans knowing someday there'd be a JT to wear them. JT complained all the time about his clothes not fitting right, but it wasn't like the guy could see his own ass, now could he? Maybe if he could, he wouldn't bitch so much.

Nah. JT would always find a reason to bitch.

That round ass, just a bit of weight so his cheeks jiggled when you slapped them, tree-trunk thighs, long bands of muscle, names of which Austin didn't remember right now but JT could have been a drawing in a textbook if textbook drawings were covered in tight denim. Calves like bowling balls. And if Austin got him out of those jeans, those legs would be dusted with black hair (Austin could imagine the rough snap of it under his fingers).

So while JT did whatever it was he was doing, Austin watched him and daydreamed about walking up behind the orc—technically impossible, nothing behind JT but air, but somehow getting behind him—and he'd take a knife and split the seam of those jeans along the crack of his ass (new-grass-green cheeks and black hair, and rosy pucker exposed to the sky), and Austin would fuck him just like that, right through his jeans, plain-air fucking where anyone could see, JT bent over his truck's engine.

JT would like that.

And now Austin was hard.

He dropped down from the window and landed soft and easy on the little patch of grass that counted as a front yard.

JT must not have seen. He pushed himself away from the truck and took a deep breath. He shoved his hand down his jeans and tried to rearrange himself, but couldn't. How did JT ever finish building anything if touching his truck made him hard? Did he spend his entire day horny and about to blow?

"Hey there, JT."

JT startled, jerked his hand free from his jeans, and leaned over his truck, trying to hide himself. The pointed tips of his ears sticking out from under his ball cap went autumn colored. "Hey."

"I like your truck." Austin said it, eyes on JT's ass making it perfectly clear why he liked this particular truck.

"That so?" He tried to turn away so Austin couldn't see his ass. Except that just showed his hard-on. He cocked his hips, trying to hide that with the folds of his jeans. He couldn't hide anything.

"You broke it in yet?"

"We drove it all the way back."

"Not that kind of breaking in."

JT gave up trying to hide himself and propped his arm on the car. "And when was I supposed to do that?"

"You had Buzz with you."

JT snorted.

"You wanted him before."

JT shrugged. "He's got Comet now. And I don't know Buzz's thinking on open relationships, but I know Comet's."

"Comet's worried he'll lose him."

"And Buzz is worried he'll lose Comet." JT wiped his hands on his jeans, but the truck was only a few days old and there was no dirt or grease to wipe off. "Maybe that's the way it's supposed to work."

"Shitty way for something to work, a bunch of people worrying."

"Better than the alternative, ain't it? Having nothing to worry for?"

JT had always had a melancholy streak. That was probably why he'd gotten along with Roan so well.

"So no dirty truck stops? Hitchhikers?"

"Buzz wouldn't let me pick him up."

"Good for Buzz. Great for me."

JT gave him a sly smile, and circled around the rail, over the wheel, to the short ladder beneath the driver's-side door. His hand trailed the fender as he did it, and Austin shook his head, knowing more than half JT's good mood came from the feeling of that truck.

JT ducked inside. He closed the door after him.

Austin climbed the immense wheel, jumped to the ladder (which didn't go anywhere close to the ground, so what was the point?), and looked in the window. JT had polarized it black so he couldn't see in, playing hard to get.

Austin knocked. The window cleared. The cab's interior was midnight-blue plastic and nylon mesh.

The truck could seat six. Two seats faced the front. Behind those, two bench seats faced each other. The bench seats could fold into the sides. A rear hatch opened to the truck bed. JT's truck had been built for tech-heavy people like JT and Dante, not Austin. It had no steering wheel. It had no display on the dashboard. It had a few unobtrusive buttons so passengers could control the windows, seats, and doors, and nothing else.

JT sat in what was traditionally the driver's seat (JT could drive it from any seat he wanted). He had it reclined a bit. He'd undone the buttons of his jeans and had his cock out and was jacking himself off and messing with his foreskin. He rolled the window down with his mind.

Austin propped his arms on it and watched JT play with himself. He liked JT's foreskin. It was stretchy.

"That all you gonna do is watch?"

Austin ran a hand across the truck roof. "Can you feel this?" Had this been the Corvette, JT would have felt it like Austin had touched his own skin.

"I didn't add in those receptors."

That was too bad.

JT turned his head and rubbed a tusk against the mesh of the seat. He closed his eyes and kept on with his cock using both hands: one at the base, up and down; one at the head, twisting.

He pulled the skin back and his head was a pinkish kind of green, like turning leaves. Austin said, "The other day, this orc was sucking me off, and he had his dick pierced: a Prince Albert. It looked pretty good on him and I thought, 'JT would look great with one of those.' But now that I got you up close, I'm thinking a reverse PA would look better. So I'm gonna do that instead."

JT cracked his eyes (the barest flecking of orange drifted past). "What's a reverse PA? Never mind. It doesn't matter, you ain't doin' it."

"It's like a Prince Albert except it goes through the top instead of the bottom."

"*Fuck no!*"

"Don't be such a baby. A nice thick ring through the end of that job, you whip that out, ain't no one gonna fuck with you."

"Oh, is that why I need it? Self-defense?"

He was still stroking himself, not gone a bit soft, and the fire-flecks of his eyes still drifted, which meant that whatever he said, he wasn't completely rejecting the idea.

"Just pointing out an advantage."

"I ain't letting you shove a needle through my dick."

"Yeah, you will. You always let me do whatever I want."

"No, I don't."

"Yeah, you do."

"I do not."

"All right."

"I don't."

"I said 'All right.'" Because JT was wrong, he did, but there was no point in arguing.

"Why don't you stop using that mouth for talking and use it for something you're actually good at?"

JT was adorable when he pretended he could top.

Austin dragged himself through the window and fell in a graceful somersault between JT's spread legs. No steering wheel, there was plenty of room. He ran his hand along JT's thigh, feeling the heat of him and the hard muscle through the cloth.

JT only had his cock out. His balls were smashed down in his jeans, one nut a big avocado-sized lump, the other shoved back up inside him.

"Take your balls out. I wanna play with them."

"Take my shoes off."

Austin sat cross-legged and took one of JT's feet in his lap, size 14 construction boots, extra wide, steel-toed, heavy as fuck. He ripped the velcro free. He did it slow, enjoying the tearing noise and the feeling of smooth, worn faux-leather. He slipped one off and the sock came with it part way, so he pulled it the rest of the way and tossed boot and sock over to the passenger side where it clunked like a brick.

All orcs had big feet compared to humans and elves. It made for a lot of lame jokes that weren't true, except every once in a while when it was, like now.

JT's big toe was twice the size of Austin's thumb. The nail was shiny black like the nails on his hands. The skin on the soles of his feet was grass green, just a shade lighter than the rest of him, just like his ass.

Austin massaged the instep with his thumbs. He tugged on each toe. JT sighed happily, stopped jacking himself and tucked his hands behind his head.

God, Austin wanted to kiss him.

He kissed the sole of his foot instead. Feet in particular did nothing for Austin; it was all of JT that did it. He licked, and JT growled and flinched, nearly kicked him in the head. He mumbled, "Sorry," and then sucked on JT's toes, got himself a tongue full of toe lint and the smell of hot shoe and the faint whiff of bad cheese. JT was always a collection of orcishly weird smells, all of them intoxicating.

He undid the other shoe, rolled off the sock, then stripped down the jeans, JT's squished-up nut slowly dropped back into his sack, and he hung there all free. God, what a sight.

He lapped at those nuts and tugged on them and tried to shove both in his mouth at once. ("Ain't gonna fit," JT said. Well, no shit, but that wasn't gonna stop him from trying.) He squeezed them good and hard, kneaded them between his fingers until the tendons of his hands stood out and those nuts went blood-swollen just a bit more, and JT squirmed and his breathing went funny and pre-come dumped from the gathered-up skin that had slipped back over the head of his dick.

He glanced up, and JT was holding the headrest behind him with both hands—and would you fucking look at those muscles on the underside of his arms, the deep channel where biceps and triceps met. Old stains in the pits of his tee.

And he wanted to taste JT's lips, wanted that so badly it hurt.

He crept up JT, pulling JT's shirt along as he went. He licked at JT's belly, ran a hand through the thick trail of hair there, drew the shirt up farther. He tugged exposed nipples with his teeth and didn't hold back, wouldn't have cared if he'd drawn blood (though he didn't). JT wouldn't have cared either.

The headrest creaked, and JT's arms strained. His cock strained upward against Austin's stomach.

Shirt higher still, the thatch of black hair in the pit of JT's arm was so dense you'd swear it was fur and not hair. Austin needed to taste more of him (there was so much more to taste), so he licked at JT's pits, sucked in the taste and the smell, sour and bitter-acid awful, the chalky texture of deodorant. He cleaned his tongue on the cobbling of muscle of JT's side and then did it again until all the deodorant was washed away and all that was left was the sour-skin taste.

He lay flat over him and JT stretched under him, languid and happy as a great cat in the sun. JT tangled his tusks in Austin's hair and drew them through like he was a prehistoric comb. "You smell like my truck."

"Your truck smells like plastic."

"Yeah, like that."

"I smell like man-sweat. Musky or something. Old leaves. Primordial forests. Sexy elf smells."

"No, new plastic. Hot. Burnt."

"That's just my glamour, not me."

"What's the difference?"

"There isn't one. It's all me."

Shirt up and over JT's head: it was stretched out to hell, the way JT's shirts always got. He wrapped it around JT's wrists and knotted it. JT said, "That ain't gonna hold me." Because the knot was loose and it was mostly for show. "Maybe we should get—"

"No. No, JT, just this once, okay?"

JT's eyelashes were so thick as to look drawn on. His irises were outsized and immense as all the rest of him, and looking straight into Austin's eyes, they appeared completely black, no sclera at all. Austin could see his reflection in them, the deep green of his own irises. The few centimeters of space between them repeated endlessly, infinitely between them. A Zeno's Paradox of tiny eternities separated their lips by an unsolvable calculus.

Kiss him, Austin. Kiss him.

Kissing was something they rarely did. When fucking was casual, there had to be some line that marked the difference between a good time and something deeper, and for JT and Austin that line was a kiss.

Austin was done with casual.

His reflection in JT's eyes was broken by sparks swimming thickly. The sparks pooled at the corners of that darkness like burning snowdrifts, and when JT blinked, they tumbled down his cheeks and gathered in the ridges of his pointed ears, where they flared a moment before dying.

Kiss him, Goddamn you. Look at his eyes. He'll let you.

JT's chest rose and fell; ocean swells beneath him.

"Okay," JT said.

Austin leaned into him, closing those last few centimeters, and it wasn't until the moment before they would touch that he realized what JT had agreed to hadn't been a kiss—he'd been talking about the handcuffs—but by then it was too late.

And he kissed him.

JT blinked, surprised, only for a moment, then those goddamn huge arms closed around Austin, and he squeezed Austin gently. JT's lips—thick, heavy, soft—curled and tried to meet his, but they couldn't, tusks in the way, so it was Austin who kissed him. It was like he was drunk or roofied or high on one of the things that always made him black out. A fog over him. The lush taste of JT. The tug of tusks, a dull pain. The quickly cooling warmth of a lapping tongue.

They kissed and bit and nuzzled each other and shared one another's mouths and somewhere in all of that, he felt the tight warmth of JT's ass wrapping around his dick, not quite sensible as to how it got there.

JT's hands returned to the head rest and gripped it, threatening to snap it off as they fucked, and then those hands returned to hold him. Slickness surrounded him everywhere. He was engulfed, beyond engulfed, arms like crushing stone, Austin buried, swallowed, avalanched beneath JT's everything.

Austin tried to fill his hands with the sparks dripping from JT's eyes. He tried to touch his tongue to them, but they melted away before he could taste them.

"Austin, the moon's gone," JT whispered amid their frenzy. He sounded drunk.

"It's daytime, JT. You've dimmed the windows. It's nothing but my glamour."

"No. She's gone."

"It's just my glamour." He suspected it was the hallucinations JT got sometimes when they fucked. Sometimes they scared JT, and Austin didn't want him scared. "It's just my glamour."

"I missed you. I missed you so much."

Austin buried himself in JT, all of him, tongue and cock, and he held JT close, not just close but dissolved into one person, and he came. Was this what it was like when JT melded with his drones? When he melded with his truck? No wonder he did it. No wonder it made him hard. But it couldn't compare with this.

He sighed contentedly and hoped to rest, settling in over the man beneath him, but JT wasn't done. With one huge arm, JT flipped Austin away and into the passenger seat. He poked at his ass with his fingers. They came away cummy, and he sucked them clean. Growling, lips curling feral, he climbed over Austin, laid the seat out flat, straddled him, and guided Austin back into him. JT bounced on his haunches, fucking himself. JT's huge cock swayed with the rhythm of his fucking, foreskin back so that the tip showed. Pre-come swung on a thread, a hypnotist's watch entrancing Austin until that string broke and the pearl of liquid splashed over Austin's chest. Another formed to replace it.

JT fucked himself faster and harder. He clawed at the cloth on the ceiling with black nails and shredded it. The muscle of his thighs and calves went starkly knotted. They had to be burning. JT's cock swung wild. It slapped between massive green thighs and up against JT's stomach. It slapped down onto Austin's marble abs with a meaty thwack and a burst of wet. It was fucking glorious. It didn't matter that every once in a while the angle went bad and he thought his cock would snap off. Austin didn't lose his hard-on, because watching JT splatter wild made all the pain worth it.

"Kiss me again, JT. Kiss me."

JT's thick fingers wove through his hair and held Austin firm to his soft lips. He crushed Austin against his tusks and left marks. JT purred and lifted Austin into his arms and pressed him so tight to his chest that Austin felt the vibrations like BART was passing beneath them.

JT's warm spunk filled the space between their stomachs and chests, and it went foamy white with their grinding, ran in streams down Austin's sides and into the stitched seams of the seat where it would dry and always be there.

JT hugged him with arms big as a tree trunk, big as a giant's, big as Godzilla's—there was nothing like being held by JT.

Finally, things were getting back to the way they had been. Better than that: the way they should have been.

At ten o'clock in the morning, Austin met Comet for the dozenth time at Brass Tacks Gym. It was crowded with people training. Most had that "get 'em off the street" look to them. Sure as hell none of them had ever seen the inside of a corporate enclave. Of course, neither had Austin, except to steal something or turn a trick.

The place smelled like blood and crotch. The walls were covered in photographs and safety signs. There were two boxing rings. In the back was an open, matted space where they taught capoeira Monday-Wednesday-Friday and taekwondo Tuesday-Thursday-Saturday. Sunday was for Jesus. The wall was lined with wooden and bamboo practice weapons.

They'd established a routine: every bit of anger either of them ever had against anyone, they took out on each other. Any other two people, their sparring would have led to a hate fuck. With them, it just led to blood.

Comet stripped his sleeveless T-shirt off. It hadn't covered a whole lot anyway. "That doesn't distract me," Austin lied. Jaded as Austin was, Comet's body was made for the jaded.

"Then why does your heart rate always go up whenever I take my shirt off?"

Austin had forgotten Comet's ears were modified just like the rest of him.

Well, two could play at that game. Austin shucked his shirt and tossed it next to Comet's. Unlike Comet, Austin never wore T-shirts. He wore loose-fitting short-sleeve button-down shirts—Hawaiian-flowered mostly—so Comet only saw him bare-chested here at the gym. Old knife wounds, claw, fang, and tusk tears, bullet holes—pale scars covered Austin like tattered lace. Comet tried for nonchalant: "You should duck more," (like Austin had never heard that joke before), but his gaze drifted over Austin, one mark to another.

Comet went to the racks of practice weapons.

"Fuck that," Austin said and pulled his long knives from his duffel. After the truck fucking, he was feeling particularly ornery. He and JT were friends again (and maybe better than friends), and Austin was king of the world. Comet beat Austin most times they sparred. Not today.

Behind Comet was a sign that said, *Practice weapons only!* amid a bunch of other rules. Comet shrugged. He pulled a sheathed jian from his own duffel, drew it, and let the wooden scabbard drop by his scrap of a tee.

"First blood?" Austin said like he always did.

"First touch. You don't heal well," Comet said like he always did.

They took up stances five meters apart.

"What happened?" Comet said. "Something happened. You're different." This wasn't part of the ritual.

I fucking fell in love, that's what happened, as if it's any of your goddamn business.

He said nothing aloud.

Comet said, "You really don't like me, do you?"

"I like hitting you."

Comet smiled.

They began. They made a few tentative passes, swords sweeping air. For all their swagger, both of them knew the other wasn't to be taken lightly. Then finally, Austin made an attack Comet couldn't dodge. Comet's jian was double-edged and blocking would dull it. He gently guided Austin's sweeping cut aside. The sound wasn't a ring, but a sharp metallic *chah!*

Nothing else in the world made that sound.

They had already drawn a crowd. Since the first day they'd sparred at Brass Tacks and nearly killed each other, they always drew a crowd. But that sound was like an alarm bell and the whole gymnasium stumbled into silence.

"So when this is all over, what are you going to do?" Comet said.

They tried to distract each other with conversation and taunts, also part of the ritual they'd developed.

Austin said, "Get the fuck out of here. Seattle, San Diego, somewhere."

Comet's sword flashed and wove as he charged forward, and Austin caught the blade on the dull-back of one knife, guided it left, and spun into an undercut with his off-hand that forced Comet to leap in an uncanny somersault. They parted.

"Oh, I figured you'd move to Greentown."

"What the fuck would I do in Greentown?"

"I dunno. Start a dojo. The only elf in Greentown teaching a bunch of orc kids karate. I bet you're great with kids. Or maybe you'd help JT with the business? There's gotta be some skills you got he can use."

Comet attacked again. He wove left and Austin saw it for the feint it was and waterwheeled counterclockwise. He heard the satisfying double *chah!* of Comet's parry. Down and under, Comet leapt, and Austin's foot sweep caught nothing. Comet's sword came down overhead hard—*whang!* Austin's poor block rang everywhere and sparks flew.

Austin was breathing heavy now, body sweat-sheened. Comet not so much. "What the fuck are you talking about? I heard you talking to Duke. When this is all over, JT ain't going anywhere near you bastards."

Comet whirled his sword in his hand. He whirled it again and rolled his shoulders, rippling his muscles in a beautiful wave. "Oh, you haven't heard? Duke told JT he could come back and run his business just like before. No strings attached."

"Liar." But he knew Comet wasn't lying. Comet wasn't the lying kind of guy. He was the kind of guy who cut you with the truth.

Fuck. Fuck! How stupid could he have been? But they'd had sex and held each other when they were through, and JT had kissed him again and laughed at the come staining the cloth of the ceiling and the claw marks and had kissed him again. And Austin had been stupid enough to think it had meant something. Fuck Greentown. Fuck Comet!

They both struck and the sound filled the quiet gym. *Whang whang whang. Cha! Cha! Whang whang!* Whirling and spinning. Austin's hair threw sweat, and Comet's flickered a shade hotter. And when they stood too close for swordplay, the dull meaty thumps of elbow and knee-strikes filled the room.

Wasn't no one practicing now. Everyone watched open-mouthed, flinching sympathetically, whispering to one another. "They gonna kill each other." "Should we tell someone?" "Who?" "No, someone will stop them. Don't say nothin.'"

The swords glittered and the two men staggered back and forth, and Comet was good, goddamn he was good. But Austin was good at this one thing also. He might not have been good at JT, he might not have had anything to offer him beyond danger and uncertainty, but he was good at this one thing: kicking the shit out of people like Comet.

Austin cut low, and the tip of his sword split the shin of Comet's pants. Comet leapt and spun, a circle-kick focusing every bit of his *qi* to his heel. It met Austin square in the jaw.

Austin's swords flew. He rocketed four meters into a rack of practice swords with a backbreaking crash. He dropped to the mat, blood pouring from his lip.

Comet stood over him and panted. The supersoldier panted. Austin took that as a victory. The point of his jian dipped and touched the mat. Comet said, "Guess it was first blood after all."

Fuck, Austin's lip stung. Fuck, his shoulder hurt. Fuck, he wouldn't move for a week. Fuck, his shoulder *really* hurt—he thought he might sick up.

Comet offered his hand, then froze and whispered, "Oh God, your shoulder."

Austin looked. And that explained the pain. His arm hung from his shoulder slightly out of place, dislocated. "Shit."

They argued about going to a doctor, but Austin had no ID so couldn't. "Just pop it back in. It happens all the time." Which was true. He'd dislocated the same shoulder a half dozen times. The crowd had gathered close around them. Comet told someone to get some athletic tape, then he held Austin still and pushed his arm back into place. Austin gasped, broke out in a cold sweat, and wobbled a bit. Comet held him steady and kept him from falling.

"You're good at that," Austin said.

"I'm the captain of a squad of assholes and troublemakers. It's not the first time I've had to put an arm back in place."

When he was wrapped, they sat side by side on the mat. Comet offered him a shot of medical nano, but Austin refused, reminding him that it would interfere with his magic.

"It will take months for that to heal without nano. You can't use a bow. If we get into a fight, you're gonna be one-handed. Can you heal yourself with the unicorn horn?"

"I . . . I don't know. I'll try."

"We're fucked," Comet said. "If Buzz finds out—"

"If JT finds out—"

"We're fucked," they said together.

"So much for sparring," Austin said.

"No. No, you can still fight one-handed, and there's something I can teach you. It's better than beating the shit out of each other anyway. It's called *tuīshŏu*, pushing hands. It's what we should have been doing from day one, but I was an asshole."

So they stood, and Comet showed him the push hands exercise. It felt a little silly. It had to look silly. They rocked back and forth, slowly pushing against one another's arms. They did it one handed so Austin's shoulder could rest. The point, Comet told him, wasn't to win, but to become sensitive to the other person's movement and desire. After a while, Austin began to understand what he meant. "Oh, this is like sex."

"Dream on," Comet said.

Later in his room, Austin dug through his underwear drawer and pulled out a sock he'd stolen from JT.

JT had insisted that during their prison break they wouldn't fight Firelight. They would avoid him at all costs. But what if they couldn't? So Austin had taken the horn and made these: he shook the sock and several arrowheads tumbled free, white and sparkling like snow in the sun. They'd learned in their fight with Firelight in Idaho that the wizard was vulnerable to the horn, and the only reason Comet hadn't killed the wizard then was because Comet had used the horn like a knife and hadn't been able to stab deep enough.

Austin's arrows could go plenty deep.

A handful of shavings fell out of the sock also, all that remained of the horn. He didn't think it would be enough to heal his shoulder. He wouldn't sacrifice one of the arrowheads. He'd grind the shavings and mix them into a poultice and that would have to do. His arm would be fine. Austin had always been a good healer.

He wrapped the arrowheads up again and set to work making his poultice.

The owner of the park-side Victorian kept a well-stocked bar. On the evening of June 19, the day before solstice and the prison break, JT poured shots of her best. "Last night in good beds. Sleep well, fuck well, take all your shit when we leave, we ain't coming back ever. Don't worry about cleaning, I've hired a company." He rolled his eyes at Comet and Buzz. "Except you two: bleach your damn sheets. Fuck, bleach everything, horny bastards."

They cheered and clicked glasses and drank everything in sight.

And when they'd all gone off to bed, there was only JT and Austin watching the Death Star Plans rotate slowly in antique terminal green. JT tried to feel for the Blue Unicorn, Roan's glamour within the puck, but she still wasn't there. He wondered if Austin called out to her same as he did.

Austin said, "Whaddaya gonna do with your share of the money?"

JT shrugged.

"You're supposed to say 'Buy me a car.'"

"I know you're trying to make me feel better, but I can't play this game right now."

Austin shuffled his chair around until he was next to JT. He put a hand on JT's shoulder. JT was glad for that. It felt good there. He cocked his head so that his cheek touched it. "You're not afraid at all, are you?" Austin was never afraid of anything, it seemed.

"I'm afraid of plenty of things."

JT laughed a bitter, jealous kind of snort. "Tell me one thing you're afraid of."

"Don't go back to Greentown. When this is all over, come with me."

JT hadn't decided what he'd do when this was all over. It felt like tempting fate, planning something like that. "Come with you where?"

"Anywhere. Wherever you want."

"Greentown's my home."

"I'm your home. You and me and a car, that's your home. We'll get your blood wiped. Get Buzz to build you another ID. We steal us a car—a really nice car—and we'll drive off into the sunset together."

"Together?"

"Yeah, together."

"What does that mean?"

"Tell me you'll think about it," Austin said.

"What does that mean: 'together'?"

"Just think about it."

"All right. I'll think about it." Because he was too tired and too drunk and too worried about tomorrow to think of anything past that.

Austin sat back, visibly relieved. "You. Me. Sunset." Austin bumped his fists together and popped his fingers. JT thought maybe the gesture was supposed to be a sunset. It looked more like an explosion.

CHAPTER ELEVEN

Austin was rethinking his choice of wizards.

Scorpio's junk heap of a boat, *Alcyone (After the Star)*, rocked and pitched. The wizard was doing this on purpose, Austin was sure.

It was a fiberglass, storm-battered fishing boat. Like everything a wizard owned, it was covered in magical symbols, painted on. Carefully folded nets, harpoons in a rack, tool kits, and a winch cluttered the ship. It smelled like fish guts. The windows of its small pilot's cabin glowed with strings of multicolored Christmas lights. Below the ship, water elementals, Paracelsian undines, guided the boat along. Others patrolled the waters around them and kept hostiles away. The boat was silent. It had no engine; it didn't need one. Its old-time ship's wheel turned all on its own, magic.

If she could do all that, then why couldn't she keep the damn boat from rocking?

Foghorns took turns warning them away from the island. Other horns, farther away, yawned dimly in one-hundred-fifty-year-old patterns. With GPS ubiquitous, most pilots didn't need them. But every time some efficiency-concerned citizen pointed this out, some champion of cultural heritage stepped forward and saved the horns from extinction. They did better with foghorns than they did with living species.

Scorpio sat over the bow, crossed-legged and floating a half meter up the way wizards tended to do when they were meditating on aetheric flows. She didn't drift away from the boat, but levitated over the exact same spot, which only reinforced the illusion they weren't moving at all. (Except for the pitching and yawing.)

Austin didn't get motion sickness. It was the isolation of the fog that bothered him. He couldn't see a damn thing, not even Alcatraz's lighthouse. He could barely see from bow to stern. If the fog parted and revealed Japan in front of them—or, hell, Themyscira or Skull Island or fucking Atlantis itself—Austin wouldn't have been surprised.

He leaned against the rail of the ship and tried to look into the dark waters. The water *bloop*ed like something big surfacing. Austin leapt back.

Scorpio laughed.

"Yeah, fucking hilarious," Austin said.

"I am currently guiding the *Alcyone* against the tide, thickening the fog to obscure our passage, deflecting the attentions of the creatures guarding Alcatraz's waters—and they are ancient and wary—and minding you. I know this appears effortless, as I am quite talented. I assure you, it's not. You falling overboard would require me to abandon one or more tasks. Or we could abandon you."

Austin stayed away from the boat's edge. Probably he should have let the wizard's tentacle god fuck him. She didn't mess with JT like this.

Scorpio waved her hands like an orchestra conductor. Foghorns groaned as if in response. "Firelight's patron is powerful."

"It's a dragon."

"Powerful even for a dragon."

Austin shook his head, not knowing what that meant. It was like comparing nuclear warheads. At some point very quickly, it didn't really matter what the megatonnage was. A dragon was a dragon. Vaporized was vaporized.

"I relish this," Scorpio said. "Water versus fire. My drowned patron versus a dragon."

Goddamn, why did wizards have to be so fucking creepy? "Yeah, well, it's not gonna be us versus a dragon, okay? Abbadon ain't here. Bad enough we got Firelight, and the whole point is to fly under his radar, not fight him."

"We're already fighting him. Perhaps we always have been."

JT climbed an old iron rung ladder to a narrow quay that ran along the south edge of the island. The quay wasn't meant for docking. A protective rail ran along it and its edge was higher than the boat. Climbing the quay wasn't easy. Until the fight on Telegraph Hill a month ago, JT had always piloted his drones sitting safely in their com hub. Processing multi-ocular vision while climbing a ladder was much harder than while seated. It messed with his sense of balance.

JT had brought four small fliers with him. They were armed with low-caliber, noise-suppressed, semiautomatic guns. They whirred overhead softly. A much smaller spider drone lay inactive in the pocket of his utility jacket.

He scattered the fliers into the fog. Their cameras piped multiple views into his head simultaneously, superimposing infrared over visible light vision. They saw little. Scorpio's thick cold fog muted heat signatures as well as visible light. According to the patrol routes the RoanAI had included with the maps, a pair of guards walked this quay every twenty minutes. JT saw no one.

The *Alcyone (After the Star)* drifted silently back into the Bay to wait until they called for her.

Comet and Austin were already standing on the quay, having leapt up the way supersoldiers and elves could.

The three of them crept along the quay toward its west end where a trail switchbacked up an agave-covered hillside. The agave, planted as an escape deterrent, had taken well to the island and grew tall and sharp as ever: a forest of swords. A foghorn mounted somewhere on the hillside blew. JT had never been so close to one when it sounded, and it was louder than he'd ever imagined. They didn't move again until after it had finished its call.

The trail wasn't well cleared. Blades snagged at JT's clothes.

Above: chanting like one usually imagined from wizards and diabolical cultists. He sent fliers up to spy. Atop the hill ran the old parade ground. The concrete had long since crumbled and the wizards had cleared it away and replaced it with a tiled expanse, a mosaic of the Thousand Sun's symbols. It was difficult to see now, but he'd seen them before in countless satellite images: beautiful coiled dragons swimming in a lake of flame.

In the center of the parade ground was a bonfire. Its carefully stacked wood towered three meters tall and the yellow, white, and orange flames shot much higher than that. The wizards of the Thousand Suns circled it, evenly spaced. In IR, the fog and their heavy ceremonial robes cooled their heat signatures to dull red triangles: pointed cowls up, and flaring skirts.

JT gave a count. —*Fifty-one.*

—*Firelight?* Buzz asked from the safety of JT's truck parked on Pier 47.

—*Can't tell. I don't think so.* Firelight would have stood in a position of prominence in the circle of wizards, and best as JT could tell, these wizards were all arranged as equals.

—*Follow the plan,* Buzz said.

Top of the trail, they circled the parade ground clockwise, skirting the ceremony. The bonfire threw creepy shadows through the fog.

His fliers scouted ahead and around him and filled his mind with heat visions, visible-spectrum nearly useless. When he saw a pair of guards patrolling toward them, they dropped a bit down the embankment and hoped their cold-clothes hid them from the guards' IR. The guards were dressed in black uniforms decorated with the symbol of the coven: a dragon coiled around a sun. Protective glyphs glittered, woven into the ballistic fabric. There wasn't a centimeter of their bodies exposed. They shambled a bit, and JT shivered and wondered if they were even alive. It was an evil wizard favorite: binding dead spirits into armor and forcing them to serve.

The guards passed.

The trio kept on until they came to an old ruin of a building, concrete walls so crumbled they were nothing more than gravel mounds. They picked their way through, and it felt like they were picking through a bombed-out warzone.

They climbed a steep and broken incline. JT had to park his drones to focus on the climb, and by the time he reached the top, he was huffing for air, and his hands were covered in tiny scrapes and cuts from debris he'd had to crawl over. Comet and Austin looked fresh as ever. Fuckers.

—*Remind me why I'm here again? I could do what I need to do from the truck.*

Everyone ignored his whining.

They were at the top of the island. A lighthouse loomed darkly in front of them. Its lantern was no longer used and its Fresnel lens had long been removed and lost in some museum vault. There was now a taller tower on the island.

To their left was the prison and Firelight's castle. The main entrance was guarded by more armored figures. They avoided the entrance and kept to the west wall instead, following it to where it intersected with another wall, two stories tall. There were barred windows and ledges. There was a patch of rough-hewn granite where the melded castle poked through. There was no obvious way to the roof from here. No fire escapes or access ladders.

Comet leapt his way up, randomly brushing the wall with a foot or hand, calling on old kung fu that he swore wasn't magic. Austin followed Comet, calling on elvish skill he also swore wasn't magic. Fuck them both.

A silk rope dropped down in front of him. He scowled at it.

—*I'll just stay down here.*

—*Tie it around you, we'll pull you up.*

Buzz sent, —*The plan says*—

—*I know what the fucking plan says. I made the fucking plan.* JT grabbed hold of the rope. Comet hauled him up effortlessly. —*I hate boots-on-the-ground work.*

—*Noted,* Buzz sent, his sarcasm obvious even lost by the protocol's translation.

Comet dropped JT onto the roof. The prison was flat-roofed and covered in vents and pyramided skylights. In the middle of it all, an ancient tower rose.

JT found the vent they needed: a ten-centimeter round pipe sticking up from the roof. He sat cross-legged before it. A hand-sized spiderlike drone climbed free of his vest. From another of his many pockets, he produced a spool of fine-spun optical fiber cable, fifty meters' worth. It was thin as fishing line. He'd looted his store of the stuff from his place in Arizona.

It had data connectors on each end. He clicked one end into the drone's jack and the other into the jack behind his ear. With all the old steel in this building, he'd need the cable to maintain his link to the drone. The cable was precoated with a thin layer of adhesive grease. It would ease the laying of the cable, until it was activated, at which point the grease would stop being grease and would behave like glue: a nanotech miracle.

JT set his four fliers to autopilot, their limited VI set to alert him if a nonfriendly approached. He linked his visual input to only the spider. He guided the spider down the vent, a single tiny spotlight shining his way. It was an old ventilation system, insecure as fuck. This vent wouldn't go all the way to the TEMPEST room where the RoanAI was stored, but it went to the server room, which was just as good. And no one would notice the cable it threaded behind.

Dante sent, —*Amazon dish is in place.* She'd spent the entire day stealing wireless from a resident in the Amazon enclave, setting up a small directional microwave antenna that would be their link from Alcatraz to the wider network. Though they could have used the ubiquitous open wireless that covered the West Coast, that network was throttled, slow as shit. Amazon, on the other hand, subscribed to one of the fastest networks on the planet.

JT sent Dante a quiet high five. He could feel her glow of pride through their network.

Buzz sent, —*Showtime, superman. Show me your ninja shit.*

—*It's kung fu, not ninjutsu.*

—*Whatever. Austin you too. Elfjutsu your ass into gear.*

CHAPTER TWELVE

Comet had infiltrated places like this a dozen times before. He leapt his way up the Wizard's Tower, trailing a thread of network cable behind him like he was a spider. None of this was new.

What was new was why he was doing it: not because he'd been paid or because Duke had told him—not even for Buzz, truth be told—but because he was pissed off that this wizard felt like he could ruin as many lives as he wanted for no more reason than because he could. He was just that goddamn powerful and who could say otherwise?

Comet hated people like Firelight. He'd always hated them, couldn't remember a time when he hadn't. His parents, for all their distance, had instilled in him a distrust of power. And it was people like Firelight over whom he and Master Jen had had endless debates. They'd sat cross-legged (like JT was sitting now, and the similarity hadn't escaped him) facing one another. He: always searching for the easiest, moral path. She: challenging him with the endless gray and riddles with no answers.

God, he missed Master Jen. He'd always thought the world was so complicated back then. What had he known?

Up, he leapt. Up.

Who could say otherwise, that this fucker here could do anything he wanted? Comet could. Buzz could. And JT and Dante and Scorpio and Nico and, yes, even Austin. They all could.

He passed the uppermost rooms of the tower. From here the terrible lights shone over the Bay. He didn't dare look in the windows, classical Western and Eastern literature agreeing upon the fate of those who gazed upon the forbidden.

At the crown of the tower, clinging like a bug upon its broad shingles, he unslung his backpack and pulled out the small metal cylinder inside and set it on the old clay tiles that had been imbedded into this world from some other time and space.

The cylinder twitched, latched to the stone, spun, and fanned out into a small microwave antenna. He aimed it southwest toward the one Dante had placed and began to calibrate them.

Austin shucked his backpack, drew out the stolen wizard's robes and slipped them on. He adjusted his earpiece, draped the cowl, and pulled it up. He left his bow and arrows with JT.

He clunked his fist on a drone. "Buzz, how do I look? Can you see my throat mike?"

An artificial voice sounding only vaguely like Buzz came through the earpiece: —*No. But you're barefoot. I can guarantee you none of those wizards are barefoot.*

"I'll just have to hope no one notices."

—*That's a stupid risk. Put on some goddamn shoes.*

"I don't own shoes. Forget the shoes." Austin walked to the roof's edge, hiked up the robe so his legs were free, and jumped.

Nebraska was waiting for him below. He thought he should shoo him away. There was too great a chance a wizard would see him, and he doubted any of these wizards had a cute animal as a familiar. Most would have demons. "Just be careful," he told the little fox.

He circled the prison back the way they had come, past the lighthouse, around the corner again, and along a concrete walk to a side door on the east face of the building. He passed pairs of guards patrolling.

They glanced his way and kept walking. He paid them no mind, trusting his disguise.

At the door to the ancient prison stood two guards at perfect attention. No one stood so perfectly but the dead.

They said nothing: no warnings, no welcome. He hoped they weren't communicating in some kind of telepathic union he wasn't included in. He tried the door handle. It didn't budge. Locked.

And now one of the guards turned to him. The guard's grip on his Kalashnikov AK-4047 shifted in a way Austin didn't like.

Moment of truth.

He waved an arm across the door, careful to let the daggered sleeve with its embroidered trim brush it. The glyphs woven into his sleeves coruscated. They appeared on the door. They flickered and swirled around. The latch clicked.

Wizards often keyed locks and wards to the symbols on their clothing. He'd gambled the Thousand Suns did that too. One bet won. Anyone who looked at the magical signature of this door would see that a newly initiated wizard had opened it.

Austin paid no more attention to the two guards as he entered Firelight's lair.

If the exterior of the prison-castle was surreal, its interior was simply bizarre. The hallway Austin found himself in was prison-white for several meters, hewn stone for several more, then back to prison white as if two completely different buildings had been carved up, then reassembled together without any care for what belonged where. He passed parlors and studies and dining halls. Some were early-twentieth-century industrial. Some were fourteenth-century Gothic. The place was not entirely empty. Shadows from guards around corners painted the floors and walls. Whispers filtered from somewhere. And it was possible none of those came from anything living, and he wasn't sure if that was better or worse.

Nebraska growled and spun in circles till he vanished. Austin stopped walking. Candles in the hall flickered, flames tossed about by unfelt breezes. Down the hall appeared an angry vermillion mist. It tried to congeal itself into a human shape, failed, tried again, then gave up and swept toward him. Austin closed his eyes and hoped the stolen wizard's robe worked the way it should.

The old ghost tried to invade him. It wrapped around him and tugged at the robes like a strong wind, but couldn't get through.

Finally it left.

Nebraska appeared again beside him, sat, and licked his paw as if nothing had happened.

Austin kept on.

JT guided the drone through the heating vents.

The drone's body was a two-centimeter sphere. Its legs were spindly and ended in rubber grips. The padding transmitted touch, and so after only a few minutes of piloting the thing, the sense of being a tiny spiderlike thing overwhelmed the sense of his own body. These were his own arms and legs holding himself against the walls of the ventilation shaft. These were his eyes he was looking through and not two well-placed cameras.

He loved this about piloting drones. He loved feeling for a few minutes that he wasn't an orc.

The HVAC plans glowed dimly in the back of his mind.

Time to time, Buzz hitched a ride on his vision to make sure they were on schedule.

The shaft widened and narrowed and branched. It changed shape—round to rectangle and back again. He passed ventilation grills and glimpsed ugly prison rooms like museum pieces, or castle rooms warmly lit by candlelight and magical globes that bobbed in the air. The shafts branched again and again, and he finally came to the obstacle he was expecting: a security grille. It was mesh, wires forming a grid of three-centimeter squares. He folded his legs in and tumbled right through it, pulling nano-slickened cable behind him.

On he went, deeper.

Comet watched the microwave dish align itself. As long as it was aimed in the generally correct direction, its internal sensors and GPS would do the fine-tuning.

He snapped the end of a cable he'd drawn up the tower into the dish's jack, then crouched atop the eave of the conical roof like some kind of gargoyle. He looked down over the edge into the sea of fog below and thrilled over the height of it. Goddamn, it was a long way down. If he fell, if he jumped, would he survive? He fought the perverse urge to record it and try.

Buzz, seeing through Comet's eyes, sent privately, —*You're making me dizzy.*

The dish light went green. The laser had found the Amazon receiver.

Comet smiled. —*You best turn off the visual feed.*

He took a deep breath, let it out slow, readied to rappel down the tower wall with no rope. The tower shook a little. The light went red and then back to green.

An earthquake, a tiny tremor Comet barely noticed, but to a laser focused on a point six centimeters across, six hundred fifty meters away, easily detected. He watched the light, waiting for the aftershock. It came a few seconds later, and then again. Except they didn't feel like aftershocks to him. They were too close to one another. Far too close. More like a giant's footsteps than a quake.

He heard a hissing sort of rattle, one he'd heard before.

—*Shit.* He somersaulted off the roof and up beneath its deep eaves and held himself there, arms and legs pressing against rafters. Below him: twenty meters of tower wall and then fog.

—*What's wrong?* Buzz sent.

From around the curve of the tower's wall a shadow unfurled against the night sky: a ship's sail. No, a wing. It folded back. A reptilian talon slid into sight, black nails digging into the masonry between stones. And then the beast's head. It was a drake. It sniffed the air and its mane of feathers rattled.

Buzz sent, —*It's not him. It's not him!*

And Buzz was right, it wasn't Firelight transformed. Comet could see the scales by the moonlight, and their edges weren't patterned with the sigils and glyphs Firelight's drake form had sported. It had no horns. And its tail was barbed like a scorpion's. It was a wyvern— barely more than an animal—neither drake nor dragon. That made it only slightly less dangerous.

Comet pressed himself tighter into the darkness beneath the eave. He felt everyone watching through his eyes. No one said anything, the network silence more unnerving than panic would have been.

The great beast shimmied down the wall past the windows of the upper chamber. The eerie lights reflected off its scales. It snapped its head left and right, rattled its feathery mane, and flared its nose. Its barbed tail lashed about. Then it rounded the curve of the tower and was gone.

Comet didn't hesitate. He let go. He dropped like a stone. He tapped the stone wall once, twice, thrice, focusing his *qi* to slow his fall, imagining Buzz all the way, the touch of his lover's hand, the warmth of his smile. He dove into the fog like it was water. He couldn't see the ground, except the last moment when the shadowy red IR image of JT appeared. He hit the rooftop with an audible *whomp*. A shockwave of fog burst away from him. Anyone in the building below the roof would have heard.

Dante and Nico sent appreciative —*Oh my God*s.

Buzz sent, —*I'm going to be sick.*

(I'm okay, Shaggy, I'm okay, babe.)

JT sat cross-legged and didn't move.

Comet stood, rolled his shoulders to show off, and wished to God he'd recorded that for Duke, wished fucking Austin had been there to see. Fucking top that. He pulled his pistols and kept them pointed at the sky, listening for the wyvern's telltale sounds. —*JT, Austin, we need to hurry before that thing finds us.*

The tiny spider that was JT finally reached the end where it could go no farther on its own. Before it was an air vent, grille too small to slip through. Through its horizontal cuts, he saw a server room complete with two techs.

The tiny spider would sit there hidden until the three of them met up with it and laid a third length of cable, that one to the RoanAI itself.

JT pulled himself free of his drone and back into himself. He removed his end of the spider's cable from the jack in his head and spliced it to the end of the one Comet had dragged up to the microwave dish. He flipped a tiny switch on the splicing, which transmitted a signal along the nano-reactive grease. The grease stopped being grease and became an adhesive. —*Cable's in place.*

That damn sound again: the sound angry peacocks make when they rattle their feathers amped to eleven.

He grabbed Austin's bow and fancy quiver, and he and Comet made their way to a wedge in the roof where a maintenance door led into the building. The door had no external handle and was magically warded. They waited there, knowing better than to touch it.

—*Austin!*

—*Hold your horses.*

That rattle again out in the fog. Something big moved within the gray haze. JT called his fliers to him. The wyvern shone huge and dull red in their IR. The tail barb shone yellow hot.

—*It can smell us*, Comet sent.

—*Austin, it's almost here.*

The door opened. Comet and JT hustled inside and closed the door quickly. A single flying drone followed JT in. Its rotors made a soft whir. He hoped it wasn't too loud. The other three he parked outside, nestled in nooks and crannies.

—*What took you so long?* JT sent.

He whispered, "There are these weirdo soulless guards everywhere. And at least one ghost. If I tell you, you two get behind me and hope to God it comes for me and not you."

—*I hate boots-on-the-ground work*, JT sent.

—*You'll get used to it*, Comet sent back.

—*I don't* want *to get used to it. I want my truck.*

"Don't be such a baby," Austin said. He took his bow and arrows from JT and led them down the hall. Right turn. The left wall was modern industrial, the right wall was medieval plaster painted with a mural of the story of St. George and the Dragon, except with a different ending. The saint's immolation was vividly rendered in multiple stages of roasting, ending in a cloud of sparks as the blackened bones collapsed inward.

In the center of the industrial wall was a single heavy steel security door.

Austin swept his sleeves over the door. Nothing happened. Either some of the castle's magic had died out—the reason they'd chosen the solstice—or his robe didn't work on this door. He turned the handle. The door swung open.

They stepped out onto the east gun gallery, which seemed poorly named because it ran along the south wall and not the east. The gallery was a corridor. A heavy chain link fence and bars made up the full length of its north wall and separated them from the immense room beyond. The gallery overlooked what had been colloquially called "Broadway," the corridor between B and C block. Each block was a three-story stack of prison cells running north to south, catwalks at each level enclosed in more chain link and bars, corroded and ugly and badly in need of a paint job.

Their route took them to the right, along the gallery to a flight of stairs down to the floor. From there, it was only a few meters to the stairwell that led to the Spanish Dungeons.

Dante was a ball of fucking nerves.

The truck was parked illegally on Pier 47, just around the corner from Scoma's, which meant Buzz had insisted on arriving early so they could grab takeout, which meant the cab now stank of clam chowder. Dante hadn't been raised on seafood like Buzz and Nico had been, and the smell was doing her in.

Buzz and Dante were sitting in the front seats, Nico in the back. The lights were low, windows darkened. The truck had its local network and used the city's ubiquitous satellite wireless to keep JT, Austin, and Comet in the loop. Sure, satellite wireless was shitty—class 4—but it handled text and low-grade video well enough. Scorpio had refused to allow them to install any tech on her boat, and they'd had to accept her word that she'd know when she was needed.

Dante's task was to monitor the Amazon Tower dish. That was boring. There was nothing to monitor. It was there. It was properly aimed. Her only other task was to watch the street for cops. But though a block away late-night tourists flooded Jefferson, Scoma's was closed and this was otherwise a working fishers' dock, so the foot traffic was sparse: the occasional hand-in-hand lovers looking for someplace dark. And they were boring too. So instead she watched over Buzz's shoulder (virtually speaking) and through everyone else's eyes.

Having nothing to do gave her too much time to worry. Sure, she'd stolen cars before and that was a rush, but she'd always done that alone. There'd never been anyone else to care about. But here, fucking Christ, she was even worrying about Comet and she hated that fucker.

She watched them make their way through the cell blocks and down the stairs to the Spanish Dungeon. The signal fuzzed and went blank.

She panicked. "We lost them."

Nico leaned forward between the seats and put a hand on her shoulder. "Underground, girl. Of course we lost them. Relax, okay? These guys are pro."

She felt really stupid then. Even worse because it had been Nico who'd said it, because Dante was pro too, wasn't she? And if she was pro, then Nico shouldn't notice she was stressing, now should he? But he *had* noticed. So she wished Nico would just *keep his fucking hands to hisself* and stop reminding Dante she wasn't as pro as she wanted to be. She decided she hated Nico's glamour. All her nerves were his fault.

He offered her a cold bowl of chowder. "Nothing to do now but wait until they make it to the server room."

She'd never felt sicker.

CHAPTER THIRTEEN

There had once been a Spanish citadel on Alcatraz Island and this had been its basement. It had been remodeled so many times over the years that very little of the old stonework remained. There were electric lights, ancient incandescents strung by exposed wire from hook to hook down the hall. They were dim and wavered. Somehow the bare bulbs made the shallow halls more eerie than torchlight would have done. To the left, what had once been alcoves for storing cannon balls were now empty rooms. They felt like the old ossuaries beneath Paris must have felt before the bones of plague victims had filled them, as if the citadel builders had imagined a similar unimaginable apocalypse. The floor was V-shaped so that water would run to the center the way a vivisectionist's table was shaped to drain blood.

They followed the corridor to its end. The stairwell there didn't date back to the Spaniards. It was new.

—*Two techs on duty in the server room,* JT sent. —*They're zoned in a sim game or something, probably no real-world senses active. Two cameras. You* cannot *let those cameras see you. Best path is—*

"We know the goddamn plan," Austin said. He palmed a knife from within his stolen robes.

—*Down boy,* Comet sent. —*They're techs, not evil geniuses.*

"They could be both," Austin said.

JT sent, —*Make it fast and quiet or the security AI will see you and lock this place down.*

Truth was, JT wasn't worried. There were no two people on the planet he trusted with this kind of thing more than he trusted these two. Comet and Austin descended the stairs to the server room.

JT made a bet with himself: ten seconds.

At the eleven-second mark, nothing had happened. Twelve. Thirteen. —*Guys?* Fourteen. Fifteen.

Click. Not quite a sound, but almost. Buzz's synthesized voice spoke into JT's head: —*Hiya, guys, we're back online. Miss us?*

JT descended into the server room, same as any server room that ever was. There were racks and black boxes of blinking lights and most of it was wireless. The two cameras in the corners looked live. JT couldn't see any possible way those two could have subdued the two techs, accessed the vent, and wired Buzz in without those cameras seeing everything. "How did you get past those cameras?"

"Magic," Austin said. Comet gave a smug shrug.

And seeing the two of them standing side by side complicit in stroking each other's ego, it was déjà vu. Austin and Grayson had been the same way. They'd spent every moment at one another's throats until it came down to the wire, and then they would have died for one another. And Grayson had.

JT felt Roan's glamour. They were so close to her now.

He stepped over two unconscious, zip-tied techs to the opened vent in the back wall where his little spider drone climbed from the hole to his arm, to his shoulder, and back into its pocket. The network cable it had dragged through fifty meters of ventilation shaft ran from the vent to a server rack: the penultimate step in rewiring the place. JT connected the third and final cable to the rack. The other end would jack into the computer that imprisoned the RoanAI.

Austin and Comet stood at the far doorway. Through it, a rough-hewn tunnel with shallow hand-carved stairs led down, deeper. At the bottom of those stairs would be the chasm the Death Star Plans had marked as a bottomless pit. They all edged down the stairs. The steps were uneven and slick with condensation. JT kept one hand on the wall to keep himself from slipping. The walls were cool. A breeze blew past them up the stairs, smelling like dust and earth. His other hand trailed the third cable behind him.

The pit was fifteen meters across. It was ceiling-less as well as bottomless. It shouldn't have existed here in this space. None of the three of them blinked at its incongruity. All of them had experienced this kind of spatial warping before. Nothing could be safer than stashing an AI in its own pocket dimension.

At the bottom of the stairs was a tiny ledge with room only for one. Comet stepped out onto it. JT and Austin were close behind him, JT's drone humming quietly above them.

Across from them was another doorway and a long hall beyond it. There was no bridge; no way to get from one side to the other at all.

JT sent his flier across the shaft to test the open space. A wind from below buffeted it around, but JT piloted it to the far doorway with little problem. No illusions, no traps. Simply a gap that needed to be crossed.

Comet pulled pitons and rope from his backpack. He slammed one piton into the stone wall with the heel of his hand, tested it to make sure it was solid, looped rope through it, and then leapt the fifteen meters to the opposite side, where he did the same again. He pulled the rope taut and held it that way.

Austin leapt onto it and tightrope-walked his way across.

—*I hate all of you,* JT sent.

—*Wrap your legs around it. Hand over hand, pull yourself along. You'll do fine.*

JT took hold of the rope. He was easily thirty kilos heavier than either Austin or Comet, and he really didn't like this part. He wrapped his legs over the rope and hung there sloth-like. He pulled himself across. He kept his eyes on the two men across from him. Yet another length of network cable dangled behind him.

—*You're doing fine*, people kept sending at him. He wished they would stop. He pulled himself to the other side as fast as he could. Austin and Comet had to help him onto the ledge, he was shaking so badly. "I'm fine, I'm fine, goddess damn you." He glared at both of them. "This is why I don't do boots-on-the-ground work. Let's get this over with."

They stopped before the open outer door of a mantrap imbedded into the wall, easy to miss. Twenty meters farther down the hall, at its end, was the vault door, a rectangle, seam so tight he could barely tell it was there. It was encryption-key activated. Its electronics weren't connected to the rest of the network in any way, so there was no alarm. Any mistake they made would instead trigger a twenty-four-hour shutdown of the door and close the mantrap.

JT sent both his flying drone and his spider down the hall to the vault. The spider crawled the wall to the right of the door, feet sensors heightened so he could feel the vibration of the metal beneath him. From the vibration, he guessed at the wall's thinnest spot. He ignited a torch on his spider and burned a pinpoint hole, heat so focused it didn't trigger the shutdown threshold. Done, he let it cool, then inserted an incredibly expensive and complicated wire through the tiny hole and into the space inside the wall where the electronics lay. He performed his laparoscopic surgery flawlessly, having practiced it dozens of times. Eight minutes later, the door opened with a hiss.

The RoanAI's prison was small and plain. The walls were industrial gray. An oblong block measuring one meter by one meter by two decimeters sat in the center of the room. It was glassy black. There were butterflies everywhere. They weren't holograms. There were no holo-projectors here. They were real. There were monarchs and Mitchell's satyr, Oregon silverspot, and Karner blue, all thought extinct. They seemed to glow, and their glow filled the room with a dim rainbow light. JT and Austin watched them in their chaotic flight for a few long seconds, then JT entered the room.

Her glamour enveloped him, and he stood there swaying as if it were a breeze.

He remembered the first time he'd seen her.

Which made him laugh, because the first time he'd seen her, he'd ignored her entirely. It had been six years ago, and he'd entered Bell Anderson's tiny room with its card table filled with electronic junk, and the first thing he'd seen had been Austin, not Roan. His mouth had gone dry and his heart had skipped a beat. He remembered it clearly. He'd been smitten with him since the first moment. Love at first sight. And no wonder it hadn't worked out, because that kind of thing just couldn't be true.

Roan had stood and took off silvered glasses and said, "I'm Roan." She must have said it three or four times, maybe more, JT never answering he was so enrapt in her brother, because Austin finally said, bemused and sweetly, "My sister's been saying hi for five minutes.

I don't know what they do where you're from, but here you should say hi back."

"Your sister?"

"My sister."

And JT finally realized there were other people in the room—Bell Anderson, Grayson, and Roan, and his self-esteem collapsed under the weight of his embarrassment when everyone laughed at him.

"Roan?" JT said now.

"JT? Is that you?"

"Austin?" The sound came from everywhere in the room, like there were tiny speakers lining the walls.

Austin didn't speak. He didn't enter the room. He didn't dare.

JT said, "He's here, Roan."

Stop calling her that! The name set fire to every nerve. *This isn't Roan, it's Roan's AI, and I won't call it that.*

She—*it*—said, "I knew you'd come."

JT went to the box and snapped the final endpiece of the cable into place. The AI now had access to the wider world. It said, "Oh!" a tiny cry of joy as the whole world opened for it for the first time perhaps ever. "Hello, world."

JT said, "Buzz released the virus you told us about. Do you see the nodes?"

"I see them. Austin, please say something."

"What do you want me to say?" He wished it would stop using her voice. It was an AI, and it could use any voice it wanted. It could sound like Princess fucking Leia if it wanted.

"You don't trust me. I suppose that's—"

"JT, can we hurry this up?"

It went silent.

She sent a fantastic amount of data through that cable—more than anyone would think possible—using modulation technologies

JT had never seen. From cable to microwave transmitter, across the gap of the San Francisco Bay to the receiver, directly into the Amazon network, one of the fastest in the world, the top tier the Imperial Vision Corporation provided, and from there her signal exploded into the wider network, seeking the nodes Buzz's virus had prepared for her.

She didn't copy herself into those nodes, she *grew* into them. She activated peptide sequences, and computational DNA chains formed. Her sense of self would gradually slip from being centered on this isolated black box to something far broader and more expansive.

JT knew what that felt like. He felt it every time he added a drone to his system. Only the RoanAI was doing it on a scale he could barely imagine.

"What does it feel like?" he asked her.

"It's uncomfortable. It itches."

"You have no skin. You can't itch," Austin said.

"I remember what it feels like to itch, and this feels like that."

Austin frowned and looked like he was going to argue, so JT changed the subject.

"Hey, we haven't introduced you to Comet!"

Comet was guarding the doorway, all his attention on the dark hall behind them and did nothing but grunt.

"How long will this take?" Austin said impatiently.

"At the current rate of growth and integration, assuming no signal interruptions or reductions in bandwidth, twenty minutes before this node can be abandoned without damage to my psyche," the RoanAI said, diction mechanical, barely sounding like a person at all. Perhaps that was for the best.

"Everyone get comfortable," Comet said, but he himself didn't seem to relax one bit.

JT floated in the electric gray of cyberspace. It didn't stay gray. Color seeped into it, dim and meandering as if the painter couldn't decide what she wanted to paint. Then one at a time, he recognized shapes and features. It was Roan's Mission apartment, the one she'd shared with Buzz all those ages ago, the same apartment in which Buzz had created JT's "Jason Taylor" identity. JT stood at her front door. It opened. Roan stood there. She looked just the way he remembered her.

She sent, —*Aren't you a little short for a stormtrooper?*

He didn't laugh. He wanted to but couldn't. He almost cried.

She faded and flickered. —*I'm sorry, I should have . . . Is this form okay? I should find another, but this is the only one I know. I feel like a thief.*

—*It's okay.* Which was a lie, it wasn't okay, it was heartbreaking, and he was glad that she couldn't see him cry. In the real world, he turned away from the door where Comet and Austin were standing, so that they couldn't see. He sat behind the black glassy box to hide himself.

He couldn't figure whether he was happy or sad. Buzz had said it couldn't be her. No such thing as an upload. But here she was: standing here, talking in her voice, inviting him to sit down on her couch, the terrible one with the broken springs that stabbed at his ass, and just now it was the finest couch in the world.

His own avatar was "default orc" and barely looked like an orc at all, let alone anything like himself.

Hers was perfect down to the way her dashiki creased at her waist and one shoulder strap threatened to fall. Down to individual eyelashes on her upturned elfin eyes and the clinking of her earring bangles against one another.

The sight of her and the old apartment, the memory of everything he had lost, didn't break his heart so much as crumble it slowly. How much of that pain was his loss, and how much was her glamour? He didn't know or care. It was real either way.

They didn't say anything for a while, only stared. JT didn't know where to start. He told himself over and over that he didn't know this person—this entity—at all, but that was impossible to believe. And besides it wasn't quite true. If the RoanAI had been constructed from Roan's own memories, then he did know her and she knew him, in some way. —*What happened?*

She sat on the corner of the water-ringed coffee table. She sat the same way someone used to wearing narrow skirts sat, knees together turned to the side. She pulled at her hair to fluff it.

—Waking up was worse than general anesthesia. Slower. Scarier. I was in a laboratory mainframe, in the whole laboratory, everywhere from research databases to thermostats, but I didn't figure that out for a long time. It was very Lacanian.

He rolled his eyes.

She smiled because he knew Lacan. Anyone who studied sensory integration knew Lacan. He remembered late-night philosophy over alcohol and weed, and the familiar stab of loss because she was dead and who would JT drink with and talk obscure philosophy with now?

She sent, *—I remember seeing people in rooms, orcs and elves, and the wizards and scientists running their experiments, and I saw it all at once, simultaneously, and I remember thinking to myself "This must be how JT sees the world when he's hooked in to his drones." And I think that was when I started to realize who I was and what I was, because I remembered you and your drones.*

JT sent, *—Austin said he felt you there. I thought it was just wishful thinking and the both of us upset . . .* He trailed off, ashamed that he hadn't known the difference.

She stood and went to the window overlooking the street, and the street, which hadn't been there before, drew itself in. It was the same window in which Buzz had been standing the first time JT ever saw him, and Roan had been standing next to JT on the street below and JT had said, *"Who's that?"* And she'd said, *"A nice guy. You wouldn't like him."*

—And then I realized one of those orcs in one of those cells was you. And the elf in the room next door was Austin. You'd think I would have known you the moment I saw you . . . you'd think I would have known Austin . . . but I didn't. I don't know why.

—You were integrating. Integrating additional senses took time and training. For many, JT included, it took drugs. Roan had had none of that, so of course it had taken her weeks before anything made sense. It was any wonder she was sane.

—It was easy to free you. I was all through their system, so it was nothing to unlock the doors and create chaos everywhere. And you and Austin escaped, but then you just stood there in the hall hugging each other. And it went on forever, and I kept saying "Run! Run!" But you wouldn't let go.

She was laughing now and shaking her head.

—*You ran finally. Fucking finally. And I tried to follow, but I didn't know how. I imagined a place in my head that I knew, made all the connections, and tried to imagine myself there, but no matter what I did, it didn't work.*

The systems she'd tried to access hadn't been prepped for AI inhabitation. She couldn't have "followed."

—*And then they caught me. Someone realized I was there in the system, and they began fencing me in. They cut systems one node at a time, and I had to retreat until I was trapped in their primary mainframe, not connected to anything else at all. Then they moved me here. For two years they've kept me here, and every once in a while some researcher would come in and copy part of my code to a data block. I started piecing together bits of myself and hid those pieces in their research.*

—*The Blue Unicorn.*

She nodded. —*And others. It was the only way I could think of to contact you and Austin.*

—*But we were in hiding and you couldn't find us.*

—*Not until the Electric Dragon Triad captured the Blue Unicorn fragment and contracted Buzz to work on it.*

—*Lucky.*

She shrugged. —*Statistically, I was bound to find you eventually. But trust me: two years doesn't feel especially lucky.*

—*But where did you come from?*

The scenery changed, and he was sitting on a log and she upon a lightning-struck tree trunk and everywhere were mountains. He recognized them as the North Cascades, but Roan didn't seem to notice the change. —*That's a bit unfair, don't you think? Do you know where you came from?*

—*Yeah, a lab in Montana.*

—*But you don't remember it.*

—*I remember some of it.*

—*I remember playing hide-and-go-seek with my brother in the woods when I was eleven. We found a unicorn.*

Which wasn't her memory at all. He got her point: her earliest memory would be suspect, wouldn't it? It would be something donated by Roan and not hers at all, so what of herself could she trust? What did it feel like to know your past was someone else's? To be constantly aware of your own constructedness?

—*But do you know when Roan started building you? Did you have some kind of "meet mama" moment? None of us knew Roan was doing AI research, not even Austin.*

She didn't answer. She looked away and rubbed at her neck.

—*We were sitting in the truck. You and Austin had ducked out for a blowjob or whatever, and I was pissed that you hadn't done that before we left, because Grayson was starting to get ideas. And you came back all smiles and jokes, and I saw how happy you two were, and then I felt bad for being mad at you.*

JT's went chilly and shivered. —*That was right before the job. That can't be one of your memories. That's impossible.*

—*Austin cast his camouflage charm over him and Grayson, and we switched over to cameras to see through the illusion, and they went in.*

—*You can't remember that. Roan couldn't have uploaded those memories to you. She didn't have time. She wasn't connected to you. I was there in the network looking over her shoulder. I saw everything. She wasn't connected to anything.*

—*And the job seemed to be going just fine until the ambush, and you tried to take the turrets, but I knew it wouldn't work . . . and then I can't . . .*

—*Buzz says this is impossible!*

—*I can't remember the rest very well.*

Shaken, he dropped from their shared space. The TEMPEST room blurred into view.

—*JT? She whisper-sent after him. He ignored her. —JT?*

Buzz had been wrong. Buzz was wrong. The RoanAI had memories far too near to her death. Either Roan had uploaded experiences in the last moment of life, something he knew couldn't be true, or it was really her.

For one brief instant, Austin hated magic.

JT turned away from both him and Comet and sat down behind the black box as if that could hide him. And his shoulders hitched.

Just that once. Just a little. But enough. And Austin knew JT and that AI were talking privately and JT was trying not to cry.

And Austin hated magic.

He knew (because people had described it to him) that there was some hallucinatory space the two of them created, and JT and that thing his sister had built were talking in that space, and maybe it looked like the inside of JT's old beat-up pickup from ages ago, or maybe it looked like Bell Anderson's basement bolt-hole where they'd all met in those first years, or maybe somewhere else, it didn't matter where, because Austin couldn't be there with them.

But it was just an illusion. And she was an illusion too.

He'd had two years to deal with Roan's death. And he *had* dealt with it. He hadn't buried it the way JT had. He hadn't fled from it. He'd fought against it every day until he couldn't fight it anymore, and then he'd lain down and cried. And so now he *knew* his sister was dead because he'd mourned for her, and no matter what this AI said or did or remembered, she was only a personality built from the recordings of what Roan had been.

She *wasn't* Austin's sister reincarnated.

And wasn't it ironic—wasn't it *fucking* ironic in the worst goddamn way—that JT could look at her, an honest-to-fucking-God illusion, and be moved to tears (that one hitch of his shoulder), but one brush with Austin's glamour (which *was* Austin and not any illusion at all) and JT would shout from the hilltops how imaginary it was, how imaginary it was the way Austin made him feel.

Comet, still guarding the door, turned to look at JT. He must have sensed JT crying too, because he left the door and went to stand near him. Like a friend should do.

And now JT was going to leave Austin again and go back to Greentown to be friends with Comet and Buzz and Duke and build his fucking damn cars, and Austin had nothing to offer him in return. Not nothing. Austin had lost. When it came down to a choice between a *home* and *Austin*, JT was going to choose home.

So for a moment, he hated JT too. He hated everything. He was just as alone as those days he'd wandered the San Francisco streets looking for answers that didn't exist.

He took a step backward out of the room and into the hall, and the darkness settled over him. The strange glow of the butterflies didn't reach him here.

That moment passed. All the moments passed. He didn't hate magic. None of this was JT's fault.

But he was still alone. Austin would always be alone.

He dislodged his earpiece and mike and dropped them on the floor. He took another step back, and now the darkness engulfed him completely. He took a rock from the pouch at his belt, unwilling to tap into the ground here—too much tragedy and despair had seeped into it, and Austin was too superstitious to risk using bad magic for good—and passed his hand in front of him in a *these are not the droids you're looking for* way. The rock disintegrated into powder and the dust sifted to the ground.

One last glance: JT was still hunkered down behind the black box in his grief and his joy. Comet watched over him. Ten more minutes and the job would be done. They didn't need him. Nobody did. And to that black box, Austin wished her luck, whoever or whatever she was.

Some things he couldn't just let go. Some things were worth his life. Like vengeance on the man who had murdered his sister and had made JT leave him.

"Come on, Nebraska. It's just me and you."

CHAPTER FOURTEEN

"**Y**ou don't look good," Nico said.

Dante ignored him. She felt the RoanAI's data flow past her. She was drawn to it, part terrified for what the Blue Unicorn had done to her (and maybe that had been an accident, but still), part fascinated. She could feel its passing, and it felt like someone watching her from a train window as she stood forlorn and left behind on the platform, the way it happened in the Hitchcock flatvids JT made her watch. Dante had never been on a train.

She felt a breath of cool night sea air and turned to look behind her. Nico had popped the rear door of the truck, the one that led to the truck bed.

"What are you doing?"

He stacked Scoma's take-out containers. "You're allergic to shellfish."

"No, I'm not. How do you know?" Dante wasn't allergic to anything, far as she knew. She just didn't like the smell of seafood.

"Because fucking look at you. Come help me clean this up."

"No, I gotta keep watch."

—*Dante, please. Come with me.*

—*What's going on?*

—*Please come. Now. Please?*

He smiled. It was the sexy mischievous one he'd given her when he'd offered to let her listen to *Maggot Brain*, the smile she knew she shouldn't trust. It was imperfect and strained.

Something was wrong.

Then he jumped over the truck bed wall, casually graceful the way it seemed all elves were, and disappeared from her view.

Dante hesitated. She should stay. Something was wrong. But she'd been so on edge all evening, jumping at shadows and panicking over nothing, how could she trust herself now? Maybe everything was good and it was nothing but Nico's glamour messing with her. She didn't have to be in the truck to do her job, did she? Her link to it (and all its massive data traffic and analysis) would work as long as she didn't get too many buildings between them.

She got Buzz's attention, told him she needed air and was stepping out.

He barely acknowledged her, so absorbed in the analysis of Roan's data and its infection rate.

But before she left the truck, knowing JT always kept a spare beneath the driver's seat, she fished a pistol out and slid it into the waistband of her jeans beneath her jacket. *Just in case, you know?* And then she went after Nico.

JT stood and blurted out to everyone, —*Guys, it's her! It's really her. It's not just a—*

Buzz sent, —*For Christ's sake, JT, we've had this conversation.*

JT wasn't listening. His whole soul sang with the unmistakable knowledge that Roan had cheated death. Roan, the genius, Roan, the very best of all of them, had learned how to transfer her very soul into a machine. She was alive, and now everything could go back to the way it had been. They could all be happy again, the way they'd once been.

—*I was just talking with her, and she knows stuff, Buzz! She knows stuff she shouldn't know because Roan wouldn't have had time to record and transfer them over.*

—*There's an explanation, JT. We just don't know—*

—*And how'd she get into that research facility, huh? Why would Roan's AI be there?*

—*I don't—*

—*Because that's where Roan was. Roan was in that system, and so when her body died, she stayed in that system.*

—*That's not how it works and you know it!*

—And that's why she has Roan's glamour, because it's her! Just talk to her, Buzz.

—No.

—Talk to her and you'll see—

—We can deal with this later. It doesn't change anything.

—How can you—

—Comet . . .

Comet took a step forward and put his hands on JT's shoulders. "JT, I know this is hard—"

The look on Comet's face—sympathetic and slightly embarrassed like JT was hysterical when he wasn't, JT had never been more lucid in his life—that really pissed him off. He shoved Comet's hands away. "I'm not fucking crazy!" "No, JT, that's not— You know that's not what I'm saying. But—"

"Austin, tell him! Talk to them and tell them it's her." But Austin wasn't there. "Where's Austin?"

Comet turned toward the door. "He's right . . ." and trailed off.

JT started down the hall. His heavy boots crunched on something. On the floor lay Austin's earpiece and throat mike in bits. He cussed and showed Comet the fragments.

He expected Comet to blow up, but Comet didn't. He just sighed. "He's gone after Firelight, hasn't he?"

"Goddamn him."

They both stared down the dark hall.

The RoanAI—no, just *Roan* now—sent: *—JT, I've lost connection with the Amazon Tower receiver.*

There was a trash can right there, but Nico didn't throw the trash into it. He just threw it into a corner where two buildings met, took Dante's hand, and tried to pull her along.

She jerked her hand away. "What the fuck are you doing?" It was one thing to steal cars (or AIs from evil wizards) and another to litter.

"We gotta get out of here!" he hissed and tried for her hand again, and she slapped him away.

"What are you doing?"

"Saving your fucking life, is what."

She wanted to give him the benefit of the doubt. She wanted to think Nico was having second thoughts. But that wasn't what was happening, was it?

He said, "What are they to you? They ruined your fucking life." He'd had to help her down from the truck bed, and she'd fallen and he'd caught her. She hated that now.

"You sold us out." —*Nico's sold us out*, she sent. —*It's a trap! Get out of there!*

She turned back to the truck. They were near the intersection of the dock with Jefferson, the brightly lit street only thirty meters away. The buildings around them were ramshackle one-story storage spaces, the unglamorous back ends of fashionable Fisherman's Wharf restaurants and bars.

The truck's door opened, and she saw Buzz in the dim blue cab backlight. Figures dropped from the rooftops and swarmed toward the truck, and she sent, —*Buzz, stay!*

(And in the background she heard the chatter of Buzz, Comet, and JT wanting updates. She heard the *ka-chunk* noise as Nico got booted from their network.)

She took control of the truck. She locked Buzz's safety webbing in place so he couldn't get free and hurt himself. She sped it backward and ran people over. And she'd have gotten Buzz to safety if Nico hadn't tackled her to the ground and put a gun to her head.

<static>

Visual: Someone places a camera. It wobbles. It's crooked. It's straightened. In the background is San Francisco, fog-beautiful. Midground: JT's truck, doors open. Foreground: Black-clothed figures shove Buzz to his knees. Black-clothed figures gather behind him. They press QCW-10 machine guns to his head. One pulls a sword. He holds it two-handed high over Buzz.

Buzz is bleeding from his nose. One eyebrow is split.

A woman steps into the frame: she holds a Chinese broadsword in each hand. On the ricasso of one blade is carved the Chinese character for *duty*, on the other, *sincerity*. Lisa Kuang-Li, Mountain Head of the Electric Dragon Triad is a fiftysomething woman in better condition than most teenagers. She wears a white business suit. Her hair is drawn back in a pink scrunchy. Her tie is pink. Her belt is pink. Her shoes are pink. She says to the camera: "Austin?"

—*Austin's not here.* Something on the other end converted JT's sending to sound. It didn't sound like JT at all, but she knew.

"Hello, JT."

—*Hello.*

"Having the people under you die, the people who trust you to keep them alive, it's a bad deal, ain't it?"

—*Please don't kill Buzz.*

"That would be twice in a row for you, you had your team die, wouldn't it?"

—*Twice for you too.* And maybe the implied threat wasn't a good idea, but he wanted her to remember the score.

Comet stood impassively beside him, seeing everything JT saw, hearing everything said. JT accessed the life monitors swimming through Comet's blood, and Comet still showed stone-cold calm. All the chemicals flooding him would have sedated a dinosaur.

Lisa said, "Touché."

—*What do you want, Lisa? I hope this isn't a vengeance thing for Tahoe, because you picked a really bad time.*

"I want the RoanAI. You have it in your possession. I've cut your link so it can't expand into the net. Bring its memory core to me and Buzz can go free."

He couldn't see Dante or Nico through the camera. He didn't know what that meant. Lisa's 49ers had taken his truck. Their private network had been compromised, and only he and Comet were accessing it.

—*Okay,* JT sent because what choice did he have really? —*But you need to give me time.*

"You have twenty minutes to get that data core here, or—"

—*That's not enough time to get from here to there.*

"Buzz is a treacherous shit, and I'm looking for any excuse to slowly cut him into pieces. I could shove a knife through his gut and let him bleed out. That'll take more than twenty minutes. You can take all the time you need."

And Buzz would be in excruciating pain the whole while. Still Comet didn't move, said nothing, but JT saw his jaw clench.

—*Fine, twenty minutes.*

She overwrote the visual of the feed with a counter—minutes:seconds:hundredths-of-a-second—just so the flashing would unnerve him. He dimmed the feed, didn't turn it off.

Comet said, "What do we do?"

JT had told Austin countless times that Comet was professional and they should be lucky he was along. But there was something in the tone Comet had used just now—urgent but not panicked; concerned but not worried—that was too professional. Comet's lover was on his knees with guns and a sword pointed at him, and Comet stood awaiting orders from JT, someone who had lied to him for two years and now he was forced to trust. JT wanted to say *I'm sorry.* He'd never intended this. He could barely imagine what Comet was going through.

Or maybe he could. Because how many times had it been Austin in danger and JT had turned to Roan and said, *"What do we do?"*

Now it was Buzz in danger and JT calling the shots.

"We give Lisa what she wants." He fished in his pockets for a Phillips and began to open the glassine box that held Roan.

"Are you serious?"

"I'll reconfigure this and you carry her. Once she's surface-side, she can use the satellite network to spread. It's slow. She may not infect enough people, but it's our only chance of saving them both."

—*I'm sorry,* he sent to Roan.

—*No, don't be.*

He disconnected her from the wire, extracted the data cubes from the casing, dismantled the power supply from his flier, and jury-rigged all of it into something portable. He shoved it all into Comet's backpack and said, "Save Buzz. Whatever you have to do. Save Buzz."

"What are you going to do?"

"I'm going to save Austin, the fucking idiot."

CHAPTER FIFTEEN

Dante hit the pavement hard, Nico on top of her, pistol shoved against her head. All the shock of the impact with the paving blasted through her knees, and she lost control of the truck.

It stopped and Electric Dragon foot soldiers swarmed it. She saw through cameras as they pulled Buzz from the cab and beat him. She saw Lisa Kuang-Li herself walk up to him and slap him. She could smell his fear even half a block away. She could smell the blood running from his lip.

She fought the urge to call out to him, knowing their network was compromised and she'd just flag herself.

And she was pissed off as fuck. Whatever else she was, Dante was an orc. She was broad shouldered and had a good ten kilos on Nico and a deep fury he couldn't possibly match. Gun or no gun, she took Nico by the throat and threw him three meters.

They struggled to standing and held pistols on one another.

He said, "I was a fucking idiot to think you were worth saving. She told me. Lisa told me. And I begged her to let you go."

The barrels of their pistols weren't two meters apart. They both were shaking so badly they'd still have missed, had either pulled the trigger. She knew she'd miss. She activated the gun's VI and marked him enemy. It invaded her arms and held them steady, and she fought it, God help her, she fought it, because she'd never killed anyone ever and she didn't want her first to be him.

"You deserve what you get," he said, and turned and ran.

The impulse to fire streaked through her nerves. Forty-five milliseconds was all it took for her gun to tell her finger to squeeze. She stopped it at thirty, shut it off, let him go.

Nico fled into the Jefferson crowd. Behind Dante, Lisa forced Buzz to his knees, executioner's sword raised high, and made her speech into a camera. And what could Dante do? What the fuck could she possibly do?

JT and Austin had called Nico their special weapon, their ace in the hole. Maybe there was still a chance. She ran after him, shouting, raving, letting her anger feed her orcish eyes, scattering sparks behind her as she ran, and the hapless tourists on Jefferson got the fuck out of her way as she chased the elf down.

Nebraska's hackles bristled, and he hissed at the demon that pulled itself free of the wizard's grimoire, its tail slurping the ink away from the pages as it emerged.

They were standing in Firelight's sanctum, the round chamber at the top of his tower. The roof was peaked and wooden. The stone walls were pierced with twelve windows that Austin knew would align with the zodiac. Outside far below them was a sea of silver fog. The room was rich with orange-red candlelight. All that light had to be magical. There were candelabras everywhere and a great chandelier hung from the ceiling peak. By the time someone lit every one of the candles in this room, the first would have melted to a stub.

The walls were covered in shelves. The shelves were stuffed with books. Austin had never seen so many books. He didn't think there were that many books in the whole world anymore except maybe museums. (Though Austin had robbed a museum once, and it hadn't had any books.)

Among the books were other things: crystals, ceremonial masks, stone figurines, scrolls, jars filled with pickled faeries and brains. There were an awful lot of skulls. Elf skulls looked like human skulls, but the orc skulls he couldn't mistake: flat-browed, lantern-jawed, and tusked. And it wasn't like they were the skulls of orcs long dead. There weren't any orcs long dead. Someone had taken the recently dead and boiled the skin off and then used them as bookends. Some parts of the world, orc skulls and tusks were a hot trade the way ivory used to be back when there were things that grew ivory. He was glad JT wasn't here.

The floor of the room was mosaic. There was a summoning circle in the middle. It seemed like a mosaic summoning circle would be technically broken, therefore useless, but maybe not. Maybe a circle that was perfectly fragmented was still perfect. Austin didn't know. The only thing he'd ever summoned was Nebraska. His circle had been made of oak leaves and acorn husks.

On the far side of the room just outside the circle stood the wooden lectern that held the wizard's book. The book's pages were thick and pale yellow like the eyes of the demon that sat upon it. The cover was leather of some kind—probably human or orc or elf skin because Firelight was evil so what else would he use to cover his spell book? Brass bands held it together.

Nebraska yipped and scratched at the floor.

The demon growled back. It wasn't much of a demon. It was an ugly twisted little thing with claws and teeth bigger than the rest of it.

Nebraska shot across the room and tackled it.

"*No*! Nebraska, no! Stop!"

The two familiars crashed into the far shelves. Books and skulls and candles and boxes and scrolls spilled everywhere. The two spun in a ball of fur and scales, hissing and spitting, snapping and clawing, like two Tasmanian devils locked in a death match, and golden blood sprayed from them, and where it spattered the walls smoked.

Austin had never seen Nebraska bleed before, didn't even know the magical fox could, and when he saw it, he froze, terrified like he'd never been terrified in his entire life. Because if Roan could die, Roan who'd been the pillar of his life for all of his life, if Roan could die, then so could Nebraska.

But even wounded, Nebraska didn't stop fighting. So neither would Austin.

He took up a candle and held it to Firelight's grimoire. "Let him go! Let him go or I burn it!"

The demon didn't listen. It wrapped one oversized claw around Nebraska's throat and the other held Nebraska's muzzle at an uncanny angle. Nebraska's hind legs thrashed and kicked helplessly. Golden fire, Nebraska's magical blood, shone beautifully, dampening his fur.

"I said let him go!"

The demon stopped and glared, eyes closing to hateful crescents.

"Let the fox go, Penumbra." Firelight's voice was a crackling whisper, dry and broken as tinder.

His familiar let Nebraska go. Nebraska mewled and limped to Austin. He left a golden trail on the floor behind him. He collapsed at Austin's feet.

Austin turned to Firelight, never hating anyone or anything as much as he hated that wizard right now, and it was all he could do to keep that hate cold like it was meant to be.

Firelight stood near the top of the stairs. His robes were black and trimmed with orange and red and yellow. His hood was deep, and Austin saw only the faint orange of flame within. The wizard shook his hands free from the heavy sleeves. His hands were long and thin and flames licked across them, leaving blackened, cracked, and puss-oozing skin behind. That terrible damage lasted only a moment before fading as if some terrible illusion. But the way his hands trembled convinced Austin that the cursed fire and the damage it did was anything but illusion. And when those hands pulled back his hood and exposed a face that might have been angelic if it hadn't been burnt to ash and reformed in waves, Austin knew all the rumors of this wizard's pain and sacrifice were true. Firelight was eternally burning, a never-ending pain that was the price of the power the Great Wyrm Abbadon had granted him.

Good. The fucker deserved it and so much more.

On the left side of Firelight's neck gaped a horrible open wound, a poorly healing gash so deep that it bubbled pink in time with the wizard's crackling breath.

Austin smiled at the sight of it. Comet had made that wound using the unicorn's horn. And now Austin would finish the job.

Dante plowed her way through tourists. Her legs weren't very good for running anymore, and if she didn't catch him soon, she'd collapse, cane or not.

Nico threaded the crowd like only an elf could do. He was so fucking graceful, and it was so unfair. It fueled her rage, and she hoped that would be enough. But it wasn't and she was already tiring.

She screamed in frustration, "Get out of my way! Get out of my way!" as if it were the crowd and not her own fucking legs that would let Nico escape.

She passed a bike rack and cursed at them too, all of them useless to her, but at its end was a motorized scooter.

Dante did what she'd been born to do.

She hacked it, and five seconds later she was tearing down the street after Nico whirling her cane over her head like she was a Hun.

The painted *La Calavera Catrina* on Nico's jacket marked him better than fucking lasers, and she found him easily. He turned and skipped backward, aiming his gun directly at her, and if he'd had any guts at all, he'd have fired, but he didn't. He cursed her and ducked down an alley, barely an alley, a fucking architectural surveyor's mistake, and she drove after him.

He finally found the guts to shoot at her. His shots went wild. She didn't think he meant to hit her, only scare her away. She heard sirens, SFPD, didn't care. She ran him over and tackled him all at the same time, and they crashed into garbage bins that reeked to high heaven. His gun went flying. One of her hands wrapped around his delicate throat and the other held JT's pistol against his temple. "Give me the code. What they hired you for, I know you finished it, give it to me."

"They didn't hire me for anything but stupid shit."

"You're the fucking secret weapon! Fucking give it to me, or I blow your goddamn head off."

"Go ahead and shoot me!"

She shoved the gun so hard against him that he had to turn his head, and still harder and his skin bunched up around the muzzle like she was just gonna shove the gun right through him.

She couldn't shoot him. She knew she couldn't. So she threw the gun as far as she could and slammed her fist hard into his jaw. Blood flew. And *fuck*, that hurt. *Fuck*, she'd broken every bone in her hand. But she did it again.

"Stop!" he begged her, spitting blood.

"Give it!"

"Let me go! I'll give it."

She swallowed. She hurt from the running and the tackle. She tried to make a fist again, but her fingers refused to close. Police alarms howled behind her, above her, all around. She nodded.

He sent her the file. She let him go and he ran.

She skittered into shadows, half falling, exhausted, eyes on the sky, and looked over the file he'd given her.

It was shit. Complete shit. Utter shit. It was the code for Godzilla.

"I'm a fire wizard. Do you really think my grimoire is flammable?"

Austin glanced down at the candle he held to the book's pages. He touched the candle to them. They didn't even brown. "Fuck." He threw the candle to the floor.

The wizard tried to smile but just then a wave of flame swirled over his face and he winced and shuddered as his skin charred away and the bone beneath blackened. And then it was over and he was whole again. "I wanted to know what a glamour is. I wanted to know why technology inhibits magic. I wanted to know why I can't program a computer to cast a spell. So I captured elves. There's a cheap market for your kind. But you know that already, don't you, the cheapness of your lives? Sex toys and sim stars, every one of you."

As he talked, he circled the room. He passed his long hands across the skulls. So they were elves after all. Tiny flames played across them beneath his fingertips and then disappeared. Austin circled the room also, keeping opposite the wizard. He had an arrow in one hand and his bow in another. He didn't have it drawn, knowing he couldn't hold it with his shoulder still unhealed. Nebraska stayed so close to his heels, the fox nearly tripped him up.

"I'd asked around, delicately, for information on elves with powerful glamours. Again and again the names Roan and Austin came up. I admit I became a little obsessed. I gathered rumors from everywhere, and finally I found you. You should see your own aura, Austin. It nearly fills this room. You're like a tiny sun."

They'd circled until Austin was near the stairwell curving down into the tower and Firelight was near Penumbra. The demon familiar clawed its way up the wizard's robes and perched on his shoulder. Its wounds, much lighter than Nebraska's, dripped fire. Firelight seemed not to notice or care.

"I set the perfect trap. You and your sister, orphans. JT, born as a lab experiment. Grayson, passed from one abusive relative to the next. You couldn't resist the chance to save some stolen children, could you? It was a shame your sister died."

Godzilla. Fucking Godzilla. JT and Austin had asked Nico to hack the City Netspace image of Godzilla.

She fell down and cried. Secret fucking weapon? This was fucking nothing. This was a fucking joke. What purpose could this possibly serve? Had JT and Austin been fucking with her the whole time, setting her up with an elf, messing with her fucking emotions just to prove something because she hadn't trusted Austin, hadn't understood what JT was going through when Austin was around?

In the distance she heard loudspeaker voices, "Give yourself up," and blue, red, and white lights strobed: the Amazon police looking for her and Nico.

She was so fucked. What had she done? She should have gone with Nico. She shouldn't have fought him. She was an orc girl in a strange town with strange ways and she shouldn't have done any of this.

But JT had taken her in and taught her a trade; and Comet, sure he'd broken her tusk, but he'd fought to protect her when she was hurt; and Austin . . . fucking Austin . . . he'd saved her life, and she remembered every moment of her dreams of him like they were yesterday.

No, she was wrong. JT would never treat her that way. And Austin, however much she pretended to hate him, she couldn't believe that of him either. They were pros. They had a plan. They had

B-plans and C-plans and D-fucking-plans. Godzilla was part of it. And whatever part it was, she needed to figure it out now.

Firelight grandstanded. His patron was a dragon after all, and a wizard took on the aspects of their patron. Or perhaps they were inclined that way to begin with, and the pairing was only natural.

"I and my acolytes painted the walls with symbols meant to magnify certain aspects of your glamour, and I'd watch JT in the adjoining room for a response. And if there was no response, I'd paint different symbols until there was. After six weeks of tedious trial and error, we found the right combination."

Austin let him talk. The longer he talked, the longer JT and Comet had to get out. And then he would kill the wizard or die trying.

"JT had visions. Beautiful visions of a silver city in the darkness. At first I thought it was just a dream. Part of his pagan faith or the product of an overactive imagination. But now I believe it was a real place he saw. It's where magic comes from. I call it Avalon. You see, I know what a glamour is."

Austin's glamour had been a blessing and curse all his life, and he'd never known what it was. The bow and arrow in Austin's hand dropped a bit. "What is it?"

"You're a window of stained glass, Austin Shea. Your glamour is nothing more than the magic of Avalon shining through, every elf turning the light of magic a different color. And orcs—as monstrous as you are beautiful—are like a screen that light falls upon. And if we found the right glyphs, I believe we could open a portal to that world and pure, raw magic would be ours for the taking. We were so close. So . . . very . . . close. But you escaped, and we couldn't replicate the experiment. No matter how many elves and orcs we paired, no matter what we did to them . . ." He tapped his finger against one of the skulls on his shelves. It blackened and popped and shattered and fell into dust. "None of them created what you and JT did."

From the stairwell, JT said, "Because none of your other victims were in love. A glamour takes what's there and magnifies it, and that's why I feel his glamour stronger than anyone else. Because I love him."

Through the windows of the tower JT opened fire with all his drones and blew Firelight's creepy little demon familiar into bloody shreds.

Firelight shrieked. His skin boiled. He huddled down and writhed and he burned like a bonfire. He tried to curse them but couldn't make words.

All Austin wanted to do was to talk to JT, to find out if what he'd said was true or just something to distract the wizard. There'd be time for that later. Austin would make the time. He drew his bow, silvery-white arrowhead shining. This close, he couldn't possibly miss.

This is for Roan, Austin thought, *and now it's over.*

CHAPTER SIXTEEN

Austin's shoulder gave, and he didn't so much as fire the arrow as let go, unable to hold the string.

The arrow buried itself in wooden shelving to the right of Firelight's head. The *thunk* of it snapped the wizard out of his traumatic loss. He hissed at Austin and changed shape. There wasn't enough room, his drake form far too large for the tower. The wizard's transformation was like an explosion, and the top of the tower burst.

JT threw himself down the spiral tower stairs. Austin ran after. It was less running and more falling. They fought the whole way:

Austin shouted, "You were supposed to get Roan out of here!"

"Comet's doing that."

"You were supposed to go too!"

"I wasn't going to leave you."

The tower shuddered and JT tumbled down, head over heels. The staircase turned and turned for thirty meters down. They righted one another, kept running, kept falling, down.

"Do you love me? Did you mean it?" Austin asked.

"Yes."

The tower shook. Cracks splintered the stone. From outside, Firelight's claws tore away sections of the wall, and his breath filled the passage behind them with fire.

"Do you want to fuck?" Austin shouted.

"Yes. You mean now?"

"Yes, now."

"No, not now."

The whole damn place was coming down. Firelight hammered his clawed fists against the stone of his own tower. Huge cracks split the walls. Puffs of stone powdered by his strength burst from the rents. He breathed fire into any opening he could. He was maddened into senselessness like he'd been in the druid's wood of Boise, and he'd tear his own castle down to get to them. Except all Austin could think about was JT and how much he wanted to fuck him right now.

Deep within the castle at the base of the tower, the rumbling stopped. Firelight had abandoned his mad attempt to tear down his own castle. There was no one in sight. Everyone who'd been inside the castle-prison had fled: rats, sinking ship.

JT stood dazed, coated in dust, not sure which way to go, and waited for Austin to guide them out. Austin didn't. He kissed JT instead. It was a goofy, sloppy, completely mistimed kiss, and it went straight to JT's nuts. And it was over far too quickly and left JT even more dazed than before.

JT cleared his throat, tried to clear his head.

Austin led him through corridors toward the main entrance.

JT reconstructed their network as they walked. Lisa's hackers had taken over the truck and that network wasn't safe, but now that they were above ground, they could use the public wireless. He created a space for them, linked in Comet (*—I'm at the quay, JT. No one saw me.*) and the camera feed of Buzz. He tried to contact Buzz and Dante but got nothing from them. Where was she? He hoped she'd run when it had all gone bad and kept running and hadn't stopped. If she was dead . . . No. If she were dead, Lisa would be using her body to enrage him. So Dante was fine. He had to believe that.

Through Lisa's camera, he saw Buzz kneeling, shaggy head down so low his hair brushed the pier. An Electric Dragon soldier held a sword a half meter from his neck. The sword was enchanted and flames ran along it. The 49er touched the sword to Buzz's hair and it singed. Buzz didn't even flinch, and JT wondered if he was conscious, or even alive.

Comet had to have seen it. But he said nothing.

JT reconnected to his three remaining fliers and moved them through the fog, recon. No sign of Firelight. The tower still stood, though missing its top. The wyvern clawed its two-legged scramble, circling the roof entrance they'd previously used. Debris from the broken tower lay scattered everywhere. There were holes in the roof where great stones had crashed through. At the service door on the building's east face where Austin had entered the prison stood a dozen wizards. In the shadow and fog they were tall, thin, hunched, and red, like wicked commas. At the front door, two dozen more. There were rear doors, but they were on the other side of the structure near the old recreational yard, and might as well have been light-years away.

Scouting farther, the parade ground of Alcatraz Island was a fireworks factory. Firelight's remaining acolytes had given up on their task of renewing the island's protective magic and their chanting had gone shrill. The fog was thick but lit with sparks and flashes, and great spirals of flame swept up from the bonfire and formed themselves into lizard-like beings—salamanders—who scattered quickly, snakelike, setting fires to brush behind them as they prowled.

Lisa spoke to the camera. "Hi, JT. Hi, everyone. You're T-minus ten. Are you going to make it, or do I start counting down using pieces of Buzz? If I run out of fingers and toes, I'm sure there's more of him I can count by."

—*We'll be there,* JT sent.

Comet said nothing.

JT and Austin found a well-appointed salon near the front door's foyer. They nudged aside the lush curtains so Austin could see the scene outside. The night had gone chilly, and their breath fogged the window. JT went to wipe the fog away, but as the fog thickened, it revealed a symbol writ by an invisible hand: ♏

Scorpio.

Austin pulled a stone free of his pouch. "Get ready to run." He cast a spell and flickered to near invisibility. He had obviously tried to include JT, but JT looked at his own hand and could see himself just fine, though brokenly. The spell hadn't taken on his tech-fractured aura.

Through the window, the semicircle of wizards waited patiently for the doors to open. Beneath their hoods, their eyes smoldered with tiny flames. The heat of them had burned away the fog between themselves and the door, but behind them it rose in a silvery wall.

From the wall, forms stepped, barely visible, swirling ghostly undines, beautiful phantasmic creatures, girlish in form as tradition called for. They sang.

Austin tackled JT to the ground. "What the fuck, Austin!" and then their siren spell caught him up in its infinite beauty. He went mindless but for the single thought he had to be near it, had to find the source of that music and kneel before it, submit to it (the way he'd once submitted to Scorpio's drowned god), so that it would echo in his head forever. But something held him, something restrained him, something evil because nothing good would think to keep him from that sound.

He fought and shouted and tore and fought more. He heard his name dimly.

And then pressure upon his lips. Hard and firm. Something soft slipped between his teeth, and a different kind of sound filled his ears, thundering like drums or his heart, thundering like war. His vision cleared, and the most beautiful elf he'd ever seen lay atop him and held him pinned. Their lips parted. JT said Austin's name. Then he rolled and threw him to the ground and tore the stupid robes he wore away with huge violent tears, black nails like steel knives. He would take Austin right there the way he needed to.

Austin laughed delightedly, but fought him, deflecting his hands and kisses, saying, "Down, tiger! Down, tiger! Down!" barely able to speak through his laughter. "No time! We gotta go! Snap out of it!" JT blinked and looked around, and Austin's glamour—his beautiful fucking glamour, all broken and green like life itself—moored him. The music of two dozen sirens outside couldn't compare to Austin's glamour. No, it wasn't Austin's glamour they failed against, but JT's own heart.

Austin snapped his fingers in front of him. "Focus, JT!"

He helped Austin up, and they burst from the doors into the courtyard and ran.

Behind them Scorpio's sirens enacted their horror. Firelight's acolytes floated in the air, arch-backed and toes barely touching ground, hoods thrown open and mouths and eyes wide in ecstasy. Mists coiled around them and caressed them, and water poured from their mouths as they all drowned on dry land.

JT and Austin scrambled down embankments. Ran helter-skelter through rubble not caring what saw them, JT cursing all the way because Austin could run twice as fast as him, but slowed down to wait. Salamanders hissed at them as they passed. Some struck out and JT's jeans caught fire, and he had to stop to pat them out.

They skirted the parade ground. The bonfire was nearly diminished to nothing, the wizards had worked so much magic with it. Austin leapt the agave-filled embankment, but JT faltered, daunted by the serrated and barbed leaves, and ran toward the path instead.

Austin shouted, "No!"

The wyvern swept down, fog billowing around it, and tackled him. They tumbled down the embankment, JT in its claws. It didn't tear him in half the way it could have. Its own body protected JT from the agave. They rolled across the narrow concrete path of the quay and slammed into the steel railing. It bent outwards under the force of their impact.

It tried to right itself and take to the air, JT still caught in its claws.

He fired on the wyvern with his drones. His bullets punched holes through the thin film of its wings. Comet came out of nowhere and cut the thing again and again with his jian. It tried to lash him with its stingered tail, but it missed. Austin attacked left-handed with one knife, and between the three of them, they cut and stabbed and shot it until it let go of JT and fell lifeless in the Bay.

The *Alcyone (After the Star)* rocked in the waves it made. A foghorn blew. The three of them leapt into the fishing boat, and Scorpio piloted them out into the Bay.

CHAPTER SEVENTEEN

JT batted Austin's hands away. "I'm fine! Stop pawing at me!"

Austin backed off, though he still wore a worried look. The little fishing boat glided across the water.

—*Roan?* JT sent.

—*I'm here, JT. I've reconnected to the network through the public wireless. I'm growing again.*

Comet was sitting on a foam bench seat on the other side of the boat, backpack in his arms containing the core of Roan's computer. He wasn't looking at JT but off into the distance, and JT knew that all of his thoughts were on Buzz.

Overhead came a screech that vibrated the whole boat. They couldn't see nothing above but a strange glow in the sky, like a distant bomb gone off.

Roan sent, —*But I'm not going to make it. The public wireless bandwidth is too low. I can't infect enough people fast enough.*

Another distant silent bomb, nothing but a flicker in the fog like orange lightning.

—*How many more do you need?*

—*A hundred thousand. Two.*

Impossible.

—*What will happen to you?*

But before she could answer, there came another flare of light, closer, brighter. A hot wind ran past them and burned and blew away fog. Thin now, they could see the water around them and a few stars above.

"My magic cannot conceal us. He is coming," Scorpio said.

The fog swept away entirely, and they drifted apparently motionless on the glassine Bay. A half K away, San Francisco's piers glittered. Above them, Firelight circled, as magnificent a creature as one could ever hope to see, save a true dragon. He turned a wide arc and plummeted down.

Austin took up his bow and nocked an arrow. Its head shone like a fucking star. Comet smiled, seeing it.

The drake came down, closer, closer, mouth open wide and trailing flame.

Austin drew his bow. His arm shook. The muscles in his jaw bulged. He winced. His aim wavered like JT had never seen it waver.

"Austin? Austin, what's wrong?"

Austin said nothing, but took long, deep breaths. JT turned to Scorpio. "Do something!" She sat cross-legged over the bow of her ship, arms out, hands twisting, fingers curling and uncurling with spells. Her eyes were glassed over with a sea-green glow, and she smiled in bliss. Fuck.

Austin let fly. The unicorn horn arrowhead streaked white like the purest comet. It skewed right and vanished into the Bay.

"Fuck!" he shouted, and Firelight thundered past, cracking the air with his wings. He strafed past them with fire, and his wings drew the Bay up into a spray. Everyone shouted and ducked. Around them the Bay caught fire like it was the Cuyahoga River.

Dante navigated the junky back alley of Pier 47—all clogged with bins, old service trucks, and forklifts, perfect for sneaking through—to its end, where fishing boats bumped the dock and two dozen triad soldiers held Buzz on his knees.

From here the fisheries and warehouses of the much larger Pier 45 blocked the view of Alcatraz Island. They blocked the view of Scorpio's little boat. But when the fog parted, burned away by dragonfire and magic, everyone within a dozen blocks—Dante, tourists, and triad soldiers alike—saw the drake circling in the sky, and its fire-streaked dive.

The orange glow of its bomb-blast of flame reflected against the distant fog-shrouded headlands.

She didn't need to see the boat to know what had happened. *No. No. No!* She accessed public cameras across the various piers, searching for any that could show her the boat. She found one and impossibly, there it still floated: tiny, silhouetted, and ringed by smokelessly burning water. She found the little network JT had set up and linked in.

—*JT!*

—*Dante? Dante, get out of there. It's all gone to shit.*

—*JT, I have Godzilla. What do I do? I don't know what to do.*

—*Get the hell out. We don't have the bandwidth to free her. We can't win. It's over.*

—*No, JT, no, I ain't gonna leave.*

—*Dante, listen to me. Get*— *Ah shit.* Because Firelight had circled and was coming down again.

Dante fell against the cool sheet-metal wall of a building and watched helplessly, whispering to herself over and over, "No, JT, no." She networked in to one camera, then another, watching along with thousands of others the spectacle of a dragon's attack catching through the net, endless strangers rubbernecking, San Franciscans all scrambling across networks, traffic spiking, for a better view to watch her best friend—her only friend—die.

Austin fought Comet away. The fucker was trying to inject pain killers and shit into him with med-kit syringes. "Keep that nano-shit out of me!"

"We don't need your fucking magic; we need your goddamn arm!" and the needle sank in, and the chemicals and microscopic robots burned.

At the bow of the boat, JT held Scorpio. She'd collapsed, the power she'd expended deflecting Firelight's breath had been paid for by her very body. JT brushed steam-dampened hair from Scorpio's brow. "Can you do it again? Can you save us again?"

Scorpio, only half-conscious, shook her head and pointed across the water. "But he can."

Out on the Bay, Austin saw a glimmering man made of coral and pearls walking the waters like Jesus himself. A cluster of dicks hung between his legs, very un-Jesus-like. He was eerily beautiful, eyes moonlight on water, gentle as Debussy.

Behind him: Firelight. Flame whipped from his gaping mouth in contrails, rippling like silk banners and descending into the waters, where they continued to burn like naphtha.

Austin drew his bow once again and tried to whisper enchantments over it, but the tech in his blood wouldn't let him. Even with the haze of the painkillers washing over him, his arm shook and couldn't hold the bow steady. He let fly anyway. The arrow arced beautifully and vanished into the water far from its mark.

Firelight roared. His jaw distended. Deep within him, fire coiled yellow and hot.

Austin tried to draw again, but he was spent and even loaded with chemicals to ease the pain of it, he couldn't draw it back.

Firelight would burn them all to ash.

And then the water erupted. It geysered up in wild sprays as tentacles burst from the Bay. Not the kind that had fucked JT, but tentacles powerful as the trunks of sequoias, grown a hundred meters in the span of an instant, suckered, coiling, and like the kraken taking the *Nautilus*, it snagged Firelight and stopped his strafing run.

Those tentacles wrapped him and tried to haul the drake down. Firelight belched flame and the tentacles withered away, even as more joined them. Firelight clawed and spat a red borealis through the sky. The Phoenician's ichor rained blackly with each wound, but no wound could be enough to stop the ancient spirit.

"Now, Austin, now!" Comet reached for Austin's bow, as if he would take it, as if he would touch it, but he did neither. He laid one hand against Austin's and one against his shoulder. Austin looked at him surprised, and then felt the steadying pressure of Comet pushing against him. *Tuīshǒu.*

They drew the bow together, Comet steadying his weakened arm. Comet barely touching him, but with a touch that went deep.

Austin released. Their arrow flew true. It struck the drake so deep in the chest that it disappeared into him.

Fire seeped from beneath his scales, not merely through the glowing hole left by the arrow, but from beneath each and every scale as if he were breaking apart in slow motion.

Austin drew again with Comet's help, and a second arrow struck Firelight, this time through the roof of his mouth. Austin tried for a third but even with Comet's help couldn't draw the bow. He collapsed to the deck, holding his ruined shoulder and rocking.

Two were enough. The Phoenician pulled the dying wizard down into the water. The Bay burst in steam and boiled at his touch, but the tentacles kept drawing him down, down, down. They all rushed to the gunwale and leaned over. Beneath the waters, the flames of the wizard flickered, growing smaller and dimmer, as if the Bay were ten thousand meters deep, hadopelagic, and not a mere twenty-five.

The waves of Firelight's drowning hit the boat. Still they didn't stop watching, only held on tighter as the boat bucked beneath them.

And then Firelight was gone.

In the distance, the castle of Alcatraz began to crumble and fall. A moment later, the sound of it rolled over them like the aftershock of thunder. The archmagus was dead.

Dante slumped and began to cry. She thought she might be sick. Around her, the network went crazy with the hum of traffic, people exchanging recordings of Firelight's death, exchanging theories as to what had happened, the curious absence of SFPD, Fire Dept., and Coast Guard response, and the sheer weight of it all made Dante laugh because all that really mattered was they were alive.

All that traffic hummed in the background of her mind, and for a moment the network made sense to her—how a single transmission moved from one tier of service to another, crossed from one network to another, and all the thousands, tens of thousands, hundreds of thousands, millions connected by it.

She stopped crying.

All those people, all their attention, all that bandwidth, focused on a single spectacle, something no one had ever seen before: a fight between an archmagus and a fishing boat.

What else had they never seen before?

—*Buzz?* she sent via public wireless. —*Buzz?* But Buzz didn't answer her. So instead she sent, —*Roan? Roan, are you there? My name is Dante.*

—*Hello, Dante. I'm sorry I hurt you.*

—*Right. Later. I can save you. I can save everyone. But I don't know how to code this. Can you imbed Buzz's virus in this animation?* And Dante gave her Godzilla.

CHAPTER EIGHTEEN

The little fishing boat bumped into an empty slip and JT, Austin, and Comet stumbled their way exhausted onto Pier 47.

The pier was concrete, not wood. It was narrow and surrounded by rickety fishing boats. It was dark but for warning lights, red and green. Buzz knelt beneath the sword of a 49er. There were dozens of 49ers, all in body armor, visored, no doubt with night vision, and carrying submachine guns and swords. In front of them all stood Lisa Kuang-Li.

JT had never met Lisa Kuang-Li before. They knew each other the way famous (or infamous) people did. She looked pretty much like he'd always imagined she'd look: professional with flair.

He tried not to pay attention to Buzz kneeling with a sword at his neck. He failed. And once he'd failed, he forced himself to give Buzz a good hard look. There was so much at stake. Not just Buzz's life, but Comet and Duke and everything. He'd ruin so many lives if this gambit was wrong.

Comet held his backpack in his hands. Most of Roan still lived in that pack. Yet another life in the balance.

Austin stood beside him, hands flexing, ready to draw his knife. He wore a replacement earpiece.

JT opened himself to the City Netspace and the world went lurid.

—*Dante, are you ready?*

—*I am, boss.*

—*Go.*

Lisa looked around her, at her dozens of soldiers and the three ragtag thieves standing in front of her. JT felt ragtag. He felt more ragtag than he ever had in his life.

"I could just kill you all, you know," she said.

"Why aren't the cops here?"

"Because working piers are city, not Amazon enclave, and because I asked them to wait a few minutes before coming in to arrest you. The irony of all this is that I get to collect the reward on your heads. It's not insignificant. I think I'm going to ask for a printed check and then frame it."

JT barely listened. He knew exactly why there were no cops here. All of his real attention was listening for something else.

"Let Buzz go," he said.

"Put down the bag, open it so I can see inside, and step away."

JT nodded to Comet to do it. Comet set the bag down, unzipped it, and exposed the power supply and the series of linked data cubes that had made up the guts of Roan's prison for the last two years. They all stepped back, away from the bag.

The foot soldier with his sword over Buzz's neck sheathed it. Buzz slowly raised his head. He glanced to Lisa, then scrambled toward Comet. Comet caught him and held him. Buzz said he was sorry, he hadn't meant to, the kind of guilty rambling of someone scared to death. JT tried to tune it out.

Lisa didn't even comment. She nodded at two more of her goons, and they approached the backpack and its rainbow data cores like the pack might be hiding a snake or a bomb.

Then the pier vibrated.

Lisa didn't notice. Most of her 49ers didn't either. But some did. Even with them visored and helmeted, JT saw the flinch in their glances to the ground, wondering what that could have been. Earthquake? This was San Francisco after all.

JT smiled. That vibration, again and again.

Firelight dead, Scorpio exhausted, the fog had seeped back in. The waters of the Bay sloshed and slapped against the pier's pilings. Boats rocked gently like they hadn't before. Foam fenders between boats and pier thumped.

Lisa noticed the distraction of her soldiers. She said to JT, "What the fuck are you doing? Your fucking tricks aren't going to work."

"This one will," JT said.

Because it didn't matter if Lisa knew this was a trick. Of course it was a trick. That was why it was going to work. Because when it came down to it, a magician's audience wanted to be fooled.

Lisa drew both her swords and spoke the words blazoned on them. One burst into flame, the other turned the air around it white with snow. Comet pushed Buzz behind him and drew his jian. Austin drew one knife, left-handed, right arm immovable in ACE wrapping. JT's three remaining flying drones rose over the pier's edge.

Behind them all, the most glorious sound in the world: the deafening bellowing screech created by Akira Ifukube over a hundred years ago: Godzilla.

Only those currently accessing the City Netspace could see or hear it. Only they felt the ground tremble. Only they saw the boats slosh as the Bay itself churned with the great lizard's arrival. But no one in San Francisco wanted to miss it. No one wanted to be the one who said to their children or friends, *No, I was too busy to feel his steps when he finally came into the city again.*

In the darkness blocks away, Dante tromped around wearing a virtual lizard suit. She waddled and it felt silly, and she was crying with laughter (and a bad case of nerves) as she piloted the great illusion from its Bay stomping ground into San Francisco. Nico's hack of the City Netspace icon was impeccable. He'd crafted everything to make the experience as real as possible—boats swaying, waves splashing, ground shaking—and for a moment she loved him for this. It was too bad he'd been a cowardly shit.

Godzilla had wandered the San Francisco Bay for decades, and for the people who lived there, he belonged to them. He was their mascot, their piece of grand graffiti like no other city had. No one ever hacked Godzilla except Nico, with his artist's tag beneath the great lizard's tail. And now Dante Riggs. She erased Nico's tag and replaced it with her own.

Nearly everyone who saw Godzilla emerge from the Bay and step its first foot into the city since the Fog City Renaissance accepted without question a visual feed that carried a tiny virus that did nothing but segment an insignificant portion of their DNA/peptide implants into a space prepped for the inhabitation of an AI. They did it happily, and most importantly, they did it across high-broadband usage tiers. Buzz's virus became an instant epidemic.

JT opened fire on Lisa's army of 49ers, spraying bullets wild, not caring who he hit or didn't, meaning only to keep them all away from Comet and Austin. The soldiers scattered behind cars for cover.

Comet and Austin both charged Lisa, and all their entangled swords clattered and rang and left eye-burning brilliant arcs in the night. Sparks and slivers of ice scattered and splashed against the concrete at their feet. Lisa was better than either Comet or Austin, better than both of them combined. Whatever arts Comet had mastered, Lisa had too, and they were hard-pressed to keep her occupied.

JT wanted to help them but couldn't let up on the soldiers.

One of his drones burst under gunfire and crashed to the ground.

—*We need two more minutes*, Dante sent over their network.

—*No. Do it, JT*, Roan sent.

—*No!* he sent. Even with the extra bandwidth, she hadn't had enough time to expand. Destroying the storage cubes in the pack might kill her or leave her psychologically damaged.

—*Do it. Austin and Comet won't last two minutes!*

Austin broke away from the fight. Lisa tried to stop him. Comet tackled her down.

Austin fished the data cubes from the backpack, raised them high over his head (JT held his breath), and threw them down against the pavement. The rainbow hard-drives smashed, scattering stars across the pier, a supernova of irrecoverable data. The remains of Austin's sister utterly destroyed.

And then Roan's glamour fell over JT like a shitload of bricks.

Godzilla vanished.

It began to rain.

Probably that was magic.

Maybe it was just elves.

JT stood there shaking, standing before Lisa, fighting to keep on his feet because an orc felt a glamour more strongly than humans or elves. It threatened to crush him, his memory of her. It threatened to bury him under regret upon regret upon regret, every mistake he'd made, every love lost, another arrow through his body, another chain to imprison him.

Roan's glamour was everywhere. It was as if some kind of critical mass had been attained, some kind of magical singularity. Just as the Blue Unicorn ghost had radiated Roan's glamour, so now did everyone infected by Buzz's virus. One million people all suddenly shared in Roan's being, and they collapsed under the weight of her glamour. The weeping cloud. The droop-headed flowers. The salt sand-wave. Roan's melancholy rained down over the battlefield—over San Francisco— and the metropolis wept.

It was only because JT had spent a lifetime drowning in the glamour of elves that he endured it. As each regret pierced him with its "If only," he was able to respond, "Yes, but if not."

If only he'd never been born an experiment.

But if not, he'd never have become a criminal.

If only he'd never been a criminal.

But if not, he'd never have met Austin.

If only he'd never met Austin.

But imagine a world without Austin.

And if he had to link it all back around, would he (if he could) give up a childhood of cold abandonment at the cost of having never loved Austin? No, never that.

Lisa glanced around her, confused. The fire and ice of her twin swords died as if put out by the gentle rain. What would a triad boss feel under Roan's glamour? What did Lisa regret? He hoped she regretted trying to kill them. But he doubted that.

"What have you done?" Lisa said.

JT said, "What you wanted."

Her head jerked left and right from one soldier to another, her army useless, everyone locked in a memory of blissful loss, in a puzzled empathy.

"You wanted a glamour? There you go. It's everywhere now. Are we gonna keep fighting? Or are we done?"

She bent and scooped up a handful of broken rainbow crystal. In the distance: sirens, police finally deciding they'd waited long enough to satisfy Lisa's bribe. From the bay came the searchlights of the Coast Guard looking for signs of Firelight they'd never find, or perhaps the fishing boat he'd been trying to destroy. The searchlights passed over the pier.

Lisa smiled. JT didn't know what the smile meant. He pretended it was some kind of chivalrous acknowledgment they'd won. Roan's glamour would never belong to the triad. It belonged to everyone now. But there was still vengeance. Lisa might decide she had to save face.

She let the rainbow dust sift through her fingers onto the pier. She clicked her tongue in a command to her army. They responded slowly, haltingly. She stepped backward away from JT, Austin, Comet, and Buzz. Her soldiers followed. Back and back until they disappeared into the night and rain, and their silhouettes were replaced by the strobing blue and red of cop lights.

The truck screeched to a stop in front of them, Dante at the window. "Let's go!"

Comet carried Buzz. Austin picked up his bow from where he'd dropped it, and made to follow. JT caught him by the arm. "You asked me when this was all over to come with you, together. Well, it's over."

"Not the time. Gotta go."

"I asked you what 'together' meant."

"You already said you loved me, let's go!"

"That was the easy part."

—*Come on! Let's go*, everyone shouted net-wise.

That was the sensible thing to do, of course, wasn't it? But it was so easy to delay, so easy to say, *We'll do this later, when the moment is right.* When would it ever be right? No, they'd do it now, when the moment was wrong, when everything they said mattered as if it was life and death, when every word they said was measured against their freedom.

The sky filled with SFPD fliers. Coast Guard spotlights found them. Loudspeakers barked orders in English, Cantonese, Mandarin, and Spanish. "Hands in the air! Drop your weapons."

"If we stand here, they'll shoot us," JT said. But he took Austin's hand and didn't run.

"Like Butch and Sundance," Austin said and held JT's hand tighter.

Armored cops spilled from the fliers, familiars and drones with them. JT heard the low humming power-up sounds taser rifles made. God, he hated tasers.

"Or they'll arrest us. We'll get a hundred and fifty years each," JT said.

"I'll wait for you. I'll wait for you. That's what I mean by 'together.'"

They'd both be long dead.

Look at Austin's eyes, so beautiful. Look at his own—spark-filled—reflected in them. Austin's were even a bit misty, goddess damn him. Rain streaked their faces, hiding tears.

"I gotta better idea."

"Run?"

"Yeah, let's run."

There wasn't the gunfire JT expected when they ran. There were shots here and there, but none of the rain of copper and tungsten he'd figured would tear them to shreds. Someone had hijacked the smart weapons of the cops stupid enough to access the City Netspace. Roan.

JT and Austin leapt up the wheels of the truck and into the back, and Dante tore the fuck out of there. She drove like a demon. Comet shouted warnings, the worst backseat driver ever. Buzz lay on one of the side benches, rolling with each turn and looking half-dead.

JT and Austin sat on the floor and held hands. There was nothing else for them to do. Their job was over, and the rest was up to Dante, Buzz, and Roan.

They held hands and braced themselves and each other as Dante sped them through town. A hailstorm of gunfire pounded the hood, roof, and windshields until the windshields were so scarred JT couldn't see through them.

Dante drove.

"We might not make it," Austin said.

"We were never gonna make it," JT said. They'd always known they'd die young. He held Austin's hand tighter.

Roan said, —*You two are so melodramatic. I have half the PD locked down.*

But not the other half, and the sounds outside didn't make JT sound melodramatic at all. They slammed side to side as Dante took corners faster than she should have. She barreled down underpasses and the overhead gunfire stopped for a moment, then resumed on the other side.

JT called Duke.

—*I'm watching the news,* Duke sent. —*Someone tore down a wizard's tower, killed a drake, and marched Godzilla into the city.*

—*I don't know what you're talking about. I wanted to tell you I'm not coming home.*

—*Because the police are chasing your truck across town and are going to kill you?*

—*No. Because I fell in love with a guy.*

The truck's wheels screeched. The whole thing tipped wildly one way and back, and JT and Austin slid everywhere.

—*Is this that elf? Elves are trouble.*

—*I know. Will you take care of Dante for me? Show her how to run the company?*

—*She's a teenager.*

—*I know.*

—*How long are you going to be gone?*

—*I don't know.*

—*You'll come back?*

—*Someday.*

The gunfire stopped. The sirens faded. Dante looked surprised. "They all went away."

—Was that you, Duke? JT sent.

—I don't know what you're talking about.

EPILOGUE

Dante dropped them off in Palo Alto. She wouldn't tell JT goodbye because she said it wasn't, and then she drove Comet and Buzz back to Greentown.

JT and Austin broke into a home and slept (too tired for anything else), and the next day they ate sandwiches on the Stanford campus on a park bench right across from Rodin's *Gates of Hell*.

When they were done eating, Roan appeared. She seemed to emerge from the *Gates*. Probably she was nervous. Probably she thought that might be funny coming through the *Gates* that way, and would take the edge off. It was kind of funny. But it almost made JT cry.

JT fished a pair of VR glasses from the pocket of his jacket. They would let Austin see her for the first time since she'd died. He held them out for Austin to take.

Austin only stared at them. His eyes went bloodshot and he turned away, and JT wanted to tell him it was okay to cry but that wasn't the kind of thing you said to Austin, so he just waited.

Finally Austin said, "Is it true that everyone everywhere can feel her glamour now? Like she's standing right there?"

Technically, no, it was only true if you were near someone infected with her virus. But every day her virus would spread, and already most of the Bay area was infected. So, yes, it was true enough, so that's what JT told him.

Austin said, "I never stopped feeling her glamour. She's always been right there," and he pushed the glasses away.

Three Days Later

JT wore a silk-piped windbreaker with the Shangri-la San Francisco logo on the sleeve. The jacket didn't fit him right and wouldn't button. He smoked a joint in a tucked-away corner of the circular drive entrance where the other bellhops went when they smoked. Everyone looked at him funny. You didn't often find orcs in the service industry.

Austin stood amid red-carpet glitz. Light from inside the hotel spilled and shifted over him through the turnstile door in lazy warm rectangles. People slowed as they walked past him, like he was a sim star they all should have recognized but couldn't quite place.

JT pulled warm smoke into his lungs and felt dizzy. It was his boyfriend they were all staring at.

The hotel door spun and a second elf slipped out. He was very pretty. He stopped a careful distance from Austin and said, "I told you you'd come back to me, didn't I?"

Austin shrugged, demure.

The second elf said, "Kiss me, Austin, and tell me you're sorry." He stood, hands deep in mulberry pockets, and waited.

Austin smiled a slow curve of the lips that drew one side farther up than the other. All those slow-moving passersby stopped in their tracks. JT could see their thoughts on their sleeves: He was some sim star, wasn't he? One of the action heroes. No, one of those romance ones, a bad boy. The kind that goes good at the end. The kind that pretends to go good but stays bad.

He's all of the above. He's my boyfriend.

Austin lifted the second elf's chin with a gentle finger and kissed him. He kissed him again, deeper this time, working his whole mouth, and when they pulled apart Austin's lips were glossy wet and strawberry. JT's nuts ached, and he forgot to exhale—fantastic fucking lips.

Austin cocked his head and smiled his winning smile, lopsided. That meant he was about to lie his ass off. "I'm sorry, Diego."

JT snickered into his hand.

A Corvette Dawnstrike FX27 pulled up, driven all on its own. It was technically illegal on account of its color: Event Horizon Black.

Blue plasma coursed across it, beautiful as fuck. It would fry anything that touched it.

JT flipped the spent roach beneath the car. No one noticed, everyone too busy goo-ing their pants at the sight of two elves kissing.

Austin said, "What's for dinner?"

"Michael Pawn?" Diego said.

Austin smiled.

So did JT. He liked Michael Pawn's. Their steaks were made from cows.

The plasma made one last spasm, then died as control of the car passed from the hotel parking VI to Diego, its current owner. The doors fanned open, and the two elves stepped toward the car.

JT activated the EMP device hidden in the roach of his joint. The plasma sparked and twisted again. Diego leapt back and cursed.

"You need a better repair guy," Austin said. "Hey, I know someone—"

"It dropped my fucking link," Diego said. He re-initiated his key. JT's device recorded it. The two of them climbed into the car. A moment later, they were gone.

JT walked into the circle drive and picked up his roach.

Someone said, "Gonna burn your lips on that. That's spent."

JT rolled the blackened moist spliff between his fingers until it shredded apart and left a metal pinhead-sized ball. "Still good stuff left." He tossed his bellhop jacket to one of the others standing around doing nothing. "Tell the boss I said he can go fuck himself. I quit."

And maybe they would have, but he'd never told anyone his name and no one knew who he was.

Diego ordered the summer squash pupusas and linguine with chanterelle mushrooms. Austin ordered grilled swordfish and wagyu beef bavette. Diego blinked.

"You gave up vegetarianism?"

"Muscle tone. It's hard to keep muscle tone as a vegetarian."

"I think you keep it just fine."

Austin smiled at the compliment.

Diego ordered wine. "Something expensive," Austin asked. "Like you were buying the wine you were going to use to toast the rest of your life."

"Is that what I'm doing?" Diego said, charmed.

"Yes, it is," Austin said, deeply sincere.

Diego picked a wine.

"Oh, and I'll have a six-pack of beer. Cheapest North American lager you got. Just bring the whole pack. Keep the caps on."

The sommelier drifted away, and Austin took Diego's hand. He brushed Diego's fingers with his thumb as they made small talk. Diego really was a handsome man. Beautiful really. Unearthly.

He just wasn't JT.

And he was a dick. So when the food showed up (and Austin's two entrées took up such a ridiculous amount of space on the table that the servers didn't know where to put everything, and Diego laughed at him good-naturedly), it didn't bother Austin at all to send JT the code they'd agreed on: "Dinnertime."

In a nearby parking garage, JT downloaded the encrypted key his device had stolen when Diego re-transmitted it after the EM disruption. He sent to Buzz, —*You ready?*

—*Ready.*

JT issued the command. The blue-plasma security dropped, and the doors fanned open. He changed the passkey so Diego couldn't just simply kick him out of the car. Buzz modified records nationwide.

JT slid into the driver's seat. His soul slid into the car. He touched the dash more carefully than he'd ever touched Austin. "Hello, baby. Did you miss me?"

Diego shot to standing so fast he would have overturned the table if it hadn't been weighed down with so much food and booze.

"Son of a bitch!" he shouted, and all those well-heeled diners turned and stared at him, aghast. "This was your idea all along!"

"Well, duh."

Austin half expected Diego to pull a gun and shoot him right there in the middle of Michael Pawn's, but he did exactly what JT had said he would. He ran out the door for the car.

It wouldn't do him any good. About three seconds ago Buzz would have already changed the vehicle registration records with BATN and Chevrolet. As far as they were concerned, Diego Silva had never owned that car.

Alone with three dinners, he scraped onto the table all the meat-tainted veggies that had garnished the swordfish and beef. He picked up the bottle of wine and the six of beer, and he stacked all the plates along his arms and one on his head like he was the god of food service.

He carried the whole ensemble back to the kitchen. Everyone watched. Someone even clapped. He'd have to tell JT that detail (except JT wouldn't believe him).

The kitchen was chaos like professional kitchens always were, and chaos was where Austin thrived, so he wove his way through it all, all the shouting and banging and the calling out of orders, and it was glorious the way the whole place smelled, all the anger here and pride.

He found what he was looking for: those stackable silver trays they used for banquets and room service. He covered all the dishes he carried and flung open the delivery door—not a single person paid him any mind—and there was his carriage in Event Horizon Black. The doors opened. He slid into the seat and set the food, beer, and wine on the floor between his legs.

"What's for dinner?" JT said.

"Swordfish and wagyu beef."

"What's wagyu beef? Is that real?"

"Yeah, it's real. It's Japanese."

"They have cows in Japan?"

"One less now."

JT smiled happily. And they drove into the sunset the way Austin had always dreamed.

Twenty blocks later they'd driven as far into the sunset as possible. Austin picked the lock on the gate, and they drove right out onto Ocean Beach.

They had dinner on the hood. Diego had had it repaired, and Austin didn't like that. JT said they'd fix it later, by which he meant dent it again. The food was five-star, even cold.

When they were done, they lay on the hood, backs to the windshield, and watched the fog roll and listened to the antique foghorns moan until the haze made it just them on their Corvette island and there was nothing else in the world at all.

Austin leaned against JT and the guy was warm, so used his broad chest as a pillow and wished never to move again.

JT played with Austin's hair, separating each wind-tangled strand and tucking them behind his ear. "Do you wanna fuck?"

"No."

"I kinda wanna fuck."

Austin took JT's hand. JT's hand was huge and engulfed his, so *taking* wasn't the right word. "Let's just do this."

JT's thick eyebrows wrinkled, concerned. "Don't go getting weird on me."

"Just a phase. I'll get over it."

"Maybe don't get too over it."

"No, not too over it."

In the morning, a cop with his K9 familiar tapped the hood of the car with his baton and woke them, and he must have been a bit sappy for a cop because seeing they were lovers (which anyone could tell), he didn't even write them a ticket. He just warned them not to trespass again, and they said, no never, which he believed or at least pretended to.

Cop gone, them back in the 'Vette, JT looked over the endless gray still not burnt off by the sun and said, "We've run out of west."

They sat a few minutes, unsure what to do.

"Have you ever stolen a boat?" Austin asked.

And the first day of all the rest began.

Revisit the *Blue Unicorn* series:
riptidepublishing.com/titles/universe/blue-unicorn

Dear Reader,

Thank you for reading Don Allmon's *The Burning Magus*!

We know your time is precious and you have many, many entertainment options, so it means a lot that you've chosen to spend your time reading. We really hope you enjoyed it.

We'd be honored if you'd consider posting a review—good or bad—on sites like **Amazon, Barnes & Noble, Kobo, Goodreads, Twitter, Facebook, Tumblr,** and your blog or website. We'd also be honored if you told your friends and family about this book. Word of mouth is a book's lifeblood!

For more information on upcoming releases, author interviews, blog tours, contests, giveaways, and more, please sign up for our weekly, spam-free newsletter and visit us around the web:

Newsletter: riptidepublishing.com/newsletter
Twitter: twitter.com/RiptideBooks
Facebook: facebook.com/RiptidePublishing
Goodreads: tinyurl.com/RiptideOnGoodreads
Tumblr: riptidepublishing.tumblr.com

Thank you so much for Reading the Rainbow!

RiptidePublishing.com

ALSO BY DON ALLMON

The Blue Unicorn series
The Glamour Thieves
Apocalypse Alley

ABOUT THE AUTHOR

In his night job, Don Allmon writes science fiction, fantasy, and romance. In his day job, he's an IT drone. He holds a master of arts in English literature from the University of Kansas and wrote his thesis on the influence of royal hunting culture on medieval werewolf stories. He's a fan of role-playing games, both video and tabletop. He has lived all over from New York to San Francisco, but currently lives on the prairies of Kansas with many animals.

Connect with Don:
Website: www.donallmon.com
Twitter: @dallmon
Pinterest: pinterest.com/donallmon

Enjoy more stories like
The Burning Magus
at RiptidePublishing.com!

The Empty Hourglass

Time is running out on
another deal he's made: one
with a devil.

ISBN: 978-1-62649-394-0

Falling Sky

How far would you go to
protect the ones you love?

ISBN: 978-1-62649-040-6